"Look, I don't wanna be rude—I mean, you're pretty and all—but I ain't interested in payin' for sex."

His blunt assumption startled a bark of laughter from Nat's lips. The thought hadn't even occurred to her. He was old enough to be her father. Hell, for all she knew, he *was* her father. She'd never met the man. "I'm a pilot."

A flush crept into his cheeks, visible even through his scruffy beard. "Sorry," he mumbled, returning his gaze to his drink.

"Don't be. I'm flattered." No one had ever mistaken her for a prostitute before. Her boyish figure didn't draw that kind of attention.

He glanced at her, but the flush remained. "Then why do you wanna talk to me?"

She nodded toward his cap. "Are you an engineer?"

"Yep."

"Any good?"

Twin lines grooved his forehead and the wariness returned. "Why you wanna know?"

"I'm looking for an engineer. A good one." And he might fit the bill. Her time with Tnaryt had honed her skills at reading people. She'd bet everything in *Gypsy*'s hold that she was sitting next to a diamond in the rough.

ARCH ALLIES

Starhawke Rogue Book One

Audrey Sharpe

Ocean Dance Press

ARCH ALLIES
© 2019 Audrey Sharpe

ISBN: 978-1-946759-73-3

Ocean Dance Press, LLC
PO Box 69901
Oro Valley AZ 85737

This is a work of fiction. Any resemblance to actual persons, living or dead, business establishments, events, or locales is entirely coincidental.

Cover art by Significant Cover

Visit the author's website at:
AudreySharpe.com

*Want more interstellar adventures? Check out
these other titles in the Starhawke Universe*

Starhawke Rogue

Arch Allies
Marked Mercenaries
Resurgent Renegades

Starhawke Rising

The Dark of Light
The Chains of Freedom
The Honor of Deceit

One

Troi.

Natasha Orlov tightened her grip on the controls as she piloted her shuttle toward the brown landmass on the planet's southern hemisphere. *Gypsy* glided along without a care in the world. Nat was a wreck.

The trembling in her hands had started shortly after they'd departed the *Starhawke*'s shuttle bay. The shaking had spread to other parts of her body the closer they came to their destination. She pressed her heels into the deck to keep her knees from bouncing.

"*You're relying on the forward thrusters too much.*"

Nat snapped her head to the right, staring at the man seated in the co-pilot's chair. "What did you say?"

Marlin Brooks stared back, a bewildered expression on his lined face. "I didn't say anything."

"But I heard—" Nat broke off, not wanting to finish the sentence. She knew what she'd heard. The voice had been talking to her for more than a year. A ghost from her past who'd taken up permanent residence in her head. "Never mind."

Marlin let out the sigh of a man who'd just been expelled from paradise. "That was the prettiest ship I've ever seen."

Nat glanced at the aft camera display, but the *Starhawke* had already disappeared from view. "You could have stayed, you know. They would have taken you back to Earth."

He lifted one shoulder in a half-hearted shrug. "No point. There's nothing for me there. I'm a fifty-eight-year-old man without family or friends." He gazed out the viewport. "At least here I'll have a job."

"For as long as you want it." She'd made that promise when she'd asked him to join her on this expedition. Providing him with a steady job salved her conscience. Well, somewhat. She could never really make up for kidnapping him from Gallows Edge and putting him at the mercy of Tnaryt the sadistic Setarip for four months. She'd helped him escape, but that didn't balance the scales. It would be like stabbing someone and then expecting gratitude for treating the wound.

Honestly, she was amazed he'd chosen to throw his lot in with her. Not that he'd been overly enthusiastic about the prospect. What was the phrase he'd used? *Better the devil you know than the one you don't?*

Of course, she hadn't revealed the full extent of her plan, either. She'd asked him to be her co-pilot for local freight runs on Troi, which would solve their current lack of funds problem. But she'd neglected to mention the real reason she'd wanted to return to the planet.

Marlin shifted in his chair to face her. "I assume you've been here before?"

"Yes." Her last visit had been... memorable. "What about you?"

"I never had a reason to. Do you have family here? Friends?"

"No family." The muscles between her shoulder blades tightened. "And I don't have friends." They were alike in that respect.

He absorbed that piece of information. "Then why Troi? What's the appeal?"

She made a show of checking their heading to buy time while she considered her answer. She hadn't expected him to start asking questions. He certainly hadn't when she'd offered him the job. "It's a busy shipping port. A lot of freight runs on and off planet. With the upgrades to *Gypsy*'s systems, we should do well."

And that brought up another point. She owed a debt to Aurora Hawke and the *Starhawke* crew for those upgrades. And for saving her life. But since she never expected to see any of them again, that debt would follow her to the grave.

"I thought you were a smuggler."

"I am when I have to be. Legitimate work is better." And less likely to attract the attention of the Feds.

"But why come all the way to Troi? You could get work anywhere."

She glanced at him in surprise. The time they'd spent together on Tnaryt's ship had convinced her he was the silent type who kept to himself. Apparently not. When he didn't have the threat of imminent death hanging over his head, he became downright chatty. And curious. Not qualities she'd anticipated in her business partner.

She blew out a breath. "Tnaryt captured me here."

The silence that greeted that statement filled the shuttle. He looked like she'd hit him with a stun gun, his mouth hanging open in a perfect "O".

It took him several seconds to find his voice. "Why would you come *back?*"

She'd asked herself that question on more than one occasion. But the answer was always the same. "I have unfinished business here."

He went silent again, which was fine with her. She needed to focus on her flying anyway. They were approaching the planet's atmosphere.

At least this time she wasn't doing an emergency dive through it.

The trembling in her hands started up again. She fought the urge to glance into the aft cameras. No one was following her. She looked anyway.

The uncluttered starscape should have soothed her. It didn't. She forced her gaze forward as *Gypsy* slid into the planet's upper atmosphere, the interaction with the shields clouding the viewport. When the visuals cleared, a sea of sand stretched below them in undulating waves to the horizon.

Her shoulders locked up, every muscle from the top of her head to the middle of her back tensing. But no proximity alarms blared. No shadows swooped down, ready to snatch them from the sky.

She sucked in air, forcing her lungs to expand and contract until her breathing evened out.

"You were flying this shuttle when he caught you, weren't you?"

She didn't turn her head. "Yes."

"How long ago?"

"A year. Give or take."

"Were you alone?"

Bam! The question hit her solar plexus like a punch. She gritted her teeth. "No."

"What hap—"

"Tnaryt didn't find him." But there was at least a fifty percent chance he'd died anyway.

Marlin looked over his shoulder into the cargo area. "He was able to hide in here?" His disbelief was evident.

As well it should be. *Gypsy* had hidden compartments—she was a smuggling shuttle, after all—but none large enough to conceal a grown man.

"No." She checked the coordinates she'd entered into *Gypsy*'s system and adjusted their course to the east.

"Then where—"

"It's a long story." One she didn't want to recount.

He folded his hands in his lap. "I'm all ears."

She tightened her grip on the controls. This was not going to plan. And she only had a few minutes before they'd reach their destination. What was she going to tell him?

She could spin a tale, of course. Lying came as easily as breathing. But she didn't want to lie to him. Not after what she'd put him through.

Taking a deep breath, she plunged in. "We were delivering contraband. I was the pilot and Isin was in charge of negotiating the price. But before we reached our rendezvous point, Tnaryt's ship appeared and shot us down. I had to ditch *Gypsy* in the dunes." She gestured in the direction they were heading. "*Gypsy* was a mess—we had to leave her behind. But Isin was injured. We didn't make it far before the Setarips circled back." Her chest constricted. "We reached the top of one of the dunes and—"

Her fingers touched a smooth surface. Kneeling on all fours, she swiped furiously, clearing a section that revealed seams and a metal plate. Her gaze darted to the left, taking in the oddly symmetrical line of the dune they were on.

"It's a ship! Find a way in!" She shoved sand by the handful, desperate to locate an entrance.

Isin worked beside her. "Here!" His shout was barely audible over the snarl of the approaching ship, but the sun's rays glinted off the hatch he'd uncovered. The one she'd tripped over.

"Nat?"

She jolted back to the present, the movement causing the yoke to jerk in her hands. Sky filled the viewport as *Gypsy's* nose pushed up.

She bit the inside of her cheek as she brought the shuttle back level. "Sorry."

Marlin's hands gripped the arms of his chair until his knuckles showed white. His pasty skin had lightened a few shades, too. "You can finish after we're on the ground."

She grimaced. "Good idea."

Neither of them spoke as *Gypsy* sailed over the endless sea, her shadow rising and falling with the flow of the dunes. Nat didn't need the display to tell her when they reached the coordinates. The purple mountains in the distance stood like silent sentinels, watching over the oddly symmetrical dune rising like the prow of a ship from the undulating waves.

Her ship.

Marlin glanced between her and the viewport, clearly perplexed as to why they were circling this particular dune. "What is it?"

"A ship. Buried in the sand."

His eyes widened. He leaned over the console, peering through the viewport at the dune, then back at the sensor readings. "How do you know? The sensors don't show anything."

"I've been on it. It's where we hid from the Setarips."

He settled back into his chair, wrinkles creasing his forehead. "But this just looks like noise." He gestured at the patchwork of dots scattered across the sensor display.

She glanced at the image. "That looks like ground mineralization."

"Ground mineralization?"

"The sand here must have a high iron content. It's producing false positive readings of metallic substances throughout the area. That would mask the sensors' ability to detect the presence of the ship underneath." Which would explain why no one had discovered it. The density of the readings was slightly more concentrated where the ship rose toward the surface, but not enough that anyone would notice if they didn't already know where to look.

"How did you find it?"

"I tripped over the hatch."

"Huh."

She could practically hear him thinking. Which is why his next question didn't come as a surprise.

"Did your shipmate, Isin, die here?"

Her throat closed to the size of a pinhole. She had to clear it twice before she could answer. "I don't know."

But after a year of waiting and wondering, she would finally find out. Just not right now. It would be stupid to investigate when the sun was up. This part of Troi wasn't patrolled very often, but she wasn't going to risk getting picked up by an overzealous Fed hours after she'd arrived. She'd spent more than enough time in lockup already.

Turning away from the dunes took effort, but she altered *Gypsy*'s flight path, guiding the shuttle toward the mountain range.

"Where are you going?"

"We'll set up base camp in the mountains."

"Base camp for what? I thought we were looking for freight runs."

"We are. We will be. But—"

"But first you want to check out that ship."

She met his gaze. "Is that a problem?" He wouldn't have to come with her. She could leave him at the camp. She should be able to get into the ship on her own. So what if she was uncomfortable with the idea of walking the still corridors alone, making her way down to the torpedo room to see if Isin was—

She slammed the lid on that thought. He wasn't down there. He'd survived. He *must* have. Otherwise the past year of unrelenting horror had been for nothing.

Marlin let out a weary sigh. "No. No problem."

One hurdle down. "Thank you."

His bushy brows lifted. "For what?"

She wasn't entirely sure. "Just... thanks."

Two

Nat set *Gypsy* down beside the banks of a fresh water stream that meandered between the high walls of a wide canyon. The jagged peaks provided pockets of shade from the intense sun, with gnarled trees and scrub brush dotting the rocky landscape.

Before leaving the cockpit, she slipped her duster off her shoulders, holstered her pistol, and strapped her new comband to her forearm. The comband was a parting gift from Aurora, and a huge improvement over the pocket comms she was used to, allowing her to keep her hands free. She hadn't explored all the extra features it included, but it would undoubtedly come in handy tonight when they returned to the ship.

Aurora had given a comband to Marlin, too, but he wasn't wearing it. He didn't seem as enamored of technology as Nat was. Or of their campsite, either.

A frown pulled at his lips as he gazed at the austere landscape. "Are you sure about this location? There's water, but I don't see much in the way of food sources."

Of course he would think of food first. He was a cook, after all. "Don't worry. We won't be scavenging." She sent the command that opened the back hatch and motioned to Marlin to follow her. "Thanks to Tnaryt, we're well stocked."

"*Tnaryt?*"

She gestured to the rows of crates strapped into the cargo hold. "He had me load all this before he—" She didn't finish the sentence. Neither of them needed the reminder.

"What's in them?"

"Enough non-perishable food to last us for months. Aurora also sent a couple temperature-controlled crates of produce from the greenhouse." Walking into the *Starhawke*'s greenhouse had been like stepping into a faery land. The fresh food had put her on sensory overload after a year of choking down the mash Tnaryt had fed them, which had tasted like pureed garbage.

Marlin rested his hands on his hips and surveyed the crates. He'd had a paunch when she'd met him, but he was lean now thanks to months of hard work and a steady diet of the hideous mash. "How's it organized?"

"It's not. That's your job."

A glimmer of enthusiasm finally brightened his expression. "I can do that." He rubbed his hands together and reached for the lid on one of the crates.

"While you're sorting our food choices, I'll set up camp." *Gypsy*'s water filtration tanks were full, but Nat wanted to confirm that the water from the river could safely be used to replenish their reserves. An abundance of fresh water was another luxury she would never take for granted.

For the next hour they worked in tandem, Nat checking the water and running it through Gypsy's purification system while Marlin created order from the jumbled chaos in the crates. When he started cooking, the tantalizing aroma of grilled vegetables filled the shuttle, making Nat's mouth water.

"Smells good," she commented as she shifted several crates, clearing room to access the foldout cots they'd be using for sleeping.

He turned from the compact stovetop, a stirring spoon in one hand. "Prepare to be amazed. One taste of this dinner and you'll be transported to an exotic world of culinary delight."

She'd never seen him so happy. It lightened the weight on her shoulders. She'd rave about his efforts even if the food tasted like old boots. "I'm looking forward to it."

Reaching for the latching mechanism, she folded out one of the cots and grabbed a stack of bedding from an interior compartment. The pillow and blanket were serviceable, not luxurious, but they were clean and odor-free. A big improvement over the pallet in the tiny cubicle she'd slept on every night on Tnaryt's ship.

"When are we going to investigate that ship of yours?"

Nat paused with a sheet in her hand. "We?" She hadn't been sure he planned to come along.

He glanced over his shoulder. "I assume that's why you asked me to join you, isn't it? To help you with whatever plan you have for that ship?"

Yep. She'd definitely underestimated him. Thankfully, he seemed more accepting of the change in plan than he had been during the flight in.

She focused on making up the cot. "I could definitely use your help, but it's your choice. You're not obligated to do anything."

"Good to know." Dishes and pans clattered. "What *do* you plan to do with that ship?"

She turned, meeting his gaze as she clutched the pillow to her chest like a shield. "I plan to get it flying again."

His brows lifted. "Is that even possible?"

"Sure."

His brows moved closer to his receding hairline.

She swallowed. "At least, I think so. When I was inside, it seemed structurally sound."

"But you have no idea what caused it to crash? Or why it was abandoned?"

"No."

He turned back to the stove. "If you can repair it, what then?"

That question she could answer. "I'll run freight. A ship like that, with *Gypsy* onboard for smaller jobs—it would be a great setup. Profitable."

"For smuggling?"

She set down the pillow. "I'll take whatever I can get."

"Including the transport of... *unwilling* cargo?"

The jab caught her off guard. So that was his concern. She should have expected it. "No. I'll never do that again."

He grabbed a couple plates from the cupboard above the stove and dished the food. "It would be tempting. Easy money."

She clenched her jaw. After what she'd put him through, she deserved this. But it still stung. "I said I'd never do that again. I meant it. Never."

He set her plate and fork on one of the crates, then sat down on another crate with his plate in his hand. "Not even if your life depended on it?"

She didn't see any aggression or accusation in his eyes, just a need for confirmation. "Not even then."

They stared at each other like two dogs facing off, trying to decide if they were dealing with friend or foe.

Whatever Marlin saw in her eyes must have satisfied him. He gave a brief nod and dug into his food. "When do we leave?"

Three

I can do this.

Nat repeated the phrase silently over and over as she guided *Gypsy* into the valley between the dunes. The shuttle's running lights illuminated the towering slope concealing the ship as they descended.

Gypsy settled onto the sand, the landing gear compensating for the uneven surface, keeping the cargo bay level.

Marlin tilted his head, staring out the viewport. "It's bigger than I expected." He glanced at her. "How many crew do you suppose it needs to fly it?"

"More than two." She met his gaze. "But we'll deal with that after we've assessed the damage." And figured out how much the repairs would cost her.

From this angle, the dune looked enormous, but she remembered four, maybe five decks. Respectable, certainly, but not overwhelming. Larger than the Setarip ship they'd lived on, but smaller than the *Starhawke.*

He gave a weary sigh. "Might as well get started."

She almost smiled. One good thing about Marlin's pessimism—it was dependable. And had provided a good distraction from her jitters.

Before leaving, she activated *Gypsy*'s aerial sensors and tied the signal into her comband. Tucked into the dune with all the mineralization, the shuttle wouldn't be able to pick up much unless a ship flew directly overhead, but better safe than sorry.

She debated keeping her duster on, but couldn't justify it. Wearing it might give her a psychological boost, but it wasn't practical while digging in sand. Her Reiter pistol, however, sat snuggly against her thigh.

She strode to the cargo section, grabbed a couple collapsible shovels and water packs from the aft supply locker, and handed one of each to Marlin. "Do you have your comband?"

He pushed back his sleeve to reveal the device fastened to his forearm. "Never used one of these before."

"Trust me, it'll spoil you for anything else." She showed him how to turn on the light feature, which provided a remarkably strong circle of light with a soft glow.

He followed her lead as they exited the shuttle, the hatch closing softly behind them.

Her boots sank into the sand, the familiar sensation pulling at her calf muscles, making her work for each stride. But at least this time a heavy wind wasn't flinging debris at her. And her companion wasn't hobbled and bleeding.

"Orlov!" Isin shouted.

Nat spun, her gaze snapping to the sky. No sign of the Setarip ship. She glanced at Isin. He hadn't moved more than a meter from the shuttle. "What's wrong?"

"I need... help."

What now? She took a few steps down the slope. "Why?"

He grimaced and gestured to his leg. "I can't walk."

She blew out a breath and retraced her steps, glaring daggers at him, even though he probably couldn't see her eyes through the visor. "Why not?"

He pointed. A trail of blood led from the shuttle's hatch to a growing puddle by his heel.

Oh. She crouched beside his leg. The black fabric covering his calf was torn and soaked through. Shrapnel must have hit him when the shuttle flipped. She couldn't see anything poking out, which meant the object was likely embedded under the skin. No wonder he'd been staggering around.

Shoving the unpleasant memory aside, she focused on climbing the dune. Her heart thumped against her ribcage as she approached the peak, but not from exertion. So much for getting rid of her anxiety.

She glanced over her shoulder at Marlin. "The hatch is in this area." Unfolding her shovel, she started digging.

He did the same, methodically working his way in the opposite direction.

Before long her shovel struck with a metallic clank. The connection sent a tremor through her arm, making her whole body quake.

"It's a ship! Find a way in!"

Nope, not going there. She blocked out the echo from her past. "Marlin, over here." She set aside her shovel and dropped to all fours, using her hand like a trowel, digging into the dune and shoving sand aside. Her palm passed over more smooth metal, but also something that wasn't metal or sand. She frowned, pushing the grit away until she'd revealed a dark strip of adhesive. Not something she remembered.

Marlin crouched beside her. "What is it?"

She cleared more sand, exposing another line of adhesive and the circular handle. Her chest constricted. "Someone's sealed the hatch."

Marlin shifted to get a better view. "Doesn't look like much. Just some adhesive." He glanced up. "This wasn't here before?"

"No." She focused on her breathing to calm her racing heart. Didn't help. "The Setarips blew the hatch and left it open."

This was bad. She could think of only two reasons someone would have sealed the hatch. To keep others out. Or to keep someone *in*.

She grabbed the shovel and started digging in earnest, getting sand all over her clothes until she'd uncovered the hatch's entire outline. Pulling a multi-tool from the pouch on her holster, she opened the small blade and cut through the adhesive strip.

With the adhesive no longer holding the hatch in place, the edges popped up, unable to sit flush in the frame because of the warped metal. The Setarips had really done a number on it.

She brushed the sand off her hands and stood, grasping the handle. The hatch didn't exactly hinge open so much as totter and tumble, pulling the handle from her grasp. The door banged against the hull with a metallic clang, held in place by one small section of the original hinge. "Item one on the repair list," she muttered.

Kneeling, she directed the light from her comband into the opening. The glow reflected off the ladder attached to the deck below. Granules of sand coated the deck, giving the surface a mottled appearance. Darker brown splotches near the base of the ladder stood out against the dull grey like—

Blood. Dried blood from Isin's leg wound.

She lifted the bottle of saline and poised it over the open wound on Isin's calf. "Fair warning. This is gonna burn like fire."

He shoved his hands into the pockets of his jacket and closed his eyes. "Go ahead."

She took a deep breath as she tilted the bottle, the liquid splashing across the open wound. He let out a yell that echoed through the empty passageway, the muscles in his neck cording and his body going rigid. But he didn't pull away.

Nat sucked in air as her vision blurred. A hand on her shoulder startled her.

"Nat? What's wrong?" Marlin peered at her, the light from his comband blinding her.

She turned away, blinking rapidly, willing her pulse back to normal. "It's... nothing. Just... bad memories."

He gave her shoulder a gentle squeeze. "Want to take a minute? Or have me go first?" He didn't sound excited by the prospect, but she appreciated the offer.

"No." She gave herself a mental shake. The past couldn't hurt her unless she let it.

Swinging onto the ladder, she descended, sand crunching under her boots when she reached the deck.

The slight tilt of the ship canted the ladder ten degrees off level, which gave Marlin some trouble when he followed her. His foot slipped halfway down and he yelped, dangling in the air.

"I've got you." She rested her hands on his waist. "Let go. You're almost touching the floor."

After a quick glance over his shoulder, he released his grip, dropping like a stone. One of his heels came down on her toe and she sucked in a breath.

He stumbled, grasping the ladder. "Did I hurt you?"

Her throbbing toe told her he was heavier than he looked, but she ignored the pain. She'd told him to let go. "Nope. I'm good."

Turning her attention to the corridor, she panned her light in both directions. The warm glow revealed familiar surroundings, although everything looked subtly different from what she remembered. It took a moment to figure out why. Last time she'd been using the ghoulish green light from a glow rod. Now she was seeing the true colors, including the markings on the walls that indicated this section of the ship housed the crew cabins.

She and Isin hadn't given the rooms a passing thought. They'd been too focused on his injury and the approaching Setarips. And then they'd fled to the lower decks to hide.

Her heartbeat fluttered and she swayed. Somewhere below was the answer to the question she'd been asking herself ever since she'd been captured. But now that she was here, she couldn't get her feet to move.

Marlin stepped into her line of sight. "Which way should we go?"

Good question. Going aft would get them to their destination quicker.

Her feet pivoted in the opposite direction. "This way."

Marlin fell into step beside her, their footfalls reverberating in the close confines. To distract herself, she read the plaques beside each door they passed, counting eight cabins, the last two marked for the captain and first mate. After that, they reached the stairwell she and Isin had stumbled down.

She paused, drawing in a slow breath. The bridge would be up the stairs to the right, but she wasn't going to waste time going there when her heart was pounding in her ears, making it impossible to focus.

Going down posed its own set of problems. "I should warn you. We'll be passing some bodies along the way."

Marlin's neck popped as he jerked around to stare at her. "W-why?"

"The original crew died here." She gestured to their surroundings. "The ship's been buried ever since."

His Adam's apple bobbed up and down. "I see." He glanced between the stairway and the empty corridor. "Can you... warn me?"

"I'll try. When I came through last time, I was running from the Setarips. I wasn't exactly taking notes on where the dead people were."

His face pinched. Her comment hadn't helped.

"Or you can wait here. I can come back for you after–"

"No! I'll go." Judging by his expression, the idea of staying in the corridor alone was even more terrifying than encountering the bodies of the dead crew.

"Okay. This way."

She stayed to the left, following the stairs down two decks.

"Do you have... any idea... where you're... going?" Isin panted as he leaned on her for support.

"As far from the hatch as possible."

She'd been operating on pure instinct when they'd stumbled down these stairs together. The experience was quite different this time.

For one thing, she was seeing details and objects that had been shrouded in darkness before, including the remnants of a cozy wine bar on the port side of C deck just past the stairs. She panned her light into the passageway up ahead. "I think one of the bodies was in this area." She glanced back at Marlin.

He looked pale, his gaze darting here, there, and everywhere, but he nodded for her to continue.

They followed the corridor, passing openings into other rooms and stepping around debris along the way. But they didn't encounter any bodies.

She halted, doing a slow three-hundred-sixty-degree turn. Hadn't they—

"What is it?" Marlin fidgeted with his comband, the light bouncing around like a ball.

When it flashed into her eyes, she reached over and rested a hand on his arm, moving the light so it wasn't shining on her face. She peered down the corridor toward the stern. "I remember bodies. At least two by this point. But—"

"They're gone?" His voice went up an octave, his eyes widening with alarm.

"Or maybe I'm remembering wrong." No reason to feed his fears. Except everything else was the same. She knew where she was. Soon they'd reach the area where she'd found the ship diagram. And beyond that, the stairs that led to the torpedo bay.

Unease scurried around in her belly like a field mouse. She pulled her pistol out of its holster.

Marlin pressed against her side, whispering in her ear. "Do you think... someone's here?" He sounded like a child asking a parent if monsters lived in the closet. Courage clearly wasn't one of his strong suits.

"Probably not." After all, the hatch had been sealed from the outside. But caution seemed wise. "Let's go." Keeping her steps as silent as possible, she crept forward.

They reached the section that displayed the ship diagram without encountering any dead crewmembers. A quick glance at the diagram confirmed she remembered the layout perfectly. So what had happened to the bodies?

She motioned Marlin forward. "Stay close."

He didn't really need the reminder. She could feel his breath brushing across the top of her ear, his feet occasionally bumping against hers. But she didn't mind. She didn't want to face this alone any more than he did.

Descending another set of stairs brought them to their destination—a small room with rows of circular compartments. She stopped outside the hatchway, her gaze riveted on one of the floor-level compartments to her left. And the trail of dried blood on the deck.

Marlin peered around her shoulder. "Is that paint?"

"Blood."

"*Blood?*" His voice squeaked.

"Yes." *Isin's blood.* And it hadn't been there when she'd left him.

She moved like a sleepwalker, crossing to the torpedo tube and kneeling in front of it. Grasping the handle, she took a deep breath and swung the door open.

Empty.

The air hissed through her clenched teeth. At least he'd made it out of the tube. But the trail of blood leading into the corridor sounded an ominous note.

"Nat?" Marlin stood just inside the hatchway, his back to the bulkhead and the light from his comband pointed out into the corridor. "Why are you—"

"This is where Isin was hiding." She cleared her throat. "But it looks like he made it out of the room." And judging by the pattern of blood drops, he'd been moving under his own power.

Marlin traced the path with the light from his comband. "Do you want to… follow it?"

No. He wasn't in the tube, but that didn't mean she wouldn't find his body decomposing somewhere else on the ship.

Except she hadn't found any other bodies so far, had she? Even if he'd died here, she might never know. Whoever had sealed the hatch appeared to have cleared out the dead crew.

"Follow me."

She kept her pistol in hand, more because it comforted her than because she thought she'd need it. The drops of blood along the deck were spaced out further as they moved away from the torpedo bay, appearing in fits and starts until they reached the aft stairwell on the starboard side.

The same stairway she'd raced up to draw the Setarips away from Isin's hiding spot.

The pattern of blood splotches changed on the stairs, telling a painful story. Clearly no one had been helping him when he'd climbed those stairs. It must have taken a long time, too, judging by how much blood had seeped onto the treads. She'd applied a pressure bandage to his leg wound, but if the bandage had come loose, he could have bled out while he'd struggled up the stairs.

She reached the landing for the next deck and continued up, her boots growing heavier with each step. She didn't want to see the finale to this drama. Isin hadn't been her friend, but for reasons of temporary insanity, she'd risked her life to save him. She'd paid for her stupidity with a year of servitude. If he hadn't survived—

The blood trail ended abruptly in a small dried puddle on the next landing. And then... nothing.

She swept the light across the landing and up the next set of stairs. *No blood.* The blood loss she'd seen shouldn't have been enough to kill him. He was a big, muscular man. And she didn't see any signs of a struggle, either.

Someone had found him.

But that didn't mean he was safe, or even alive. Best-case scenario, Mirko had returned after the Feds had chased off the Setarips. Her former captain hadn't been very sympathetic to their plight when they'd contacted her while hiding in the ship, but she might have reconsidered the wisdom of abandoning her negotiator. After all, Isin had made the *Sphinx* profitable. And Mirko was all about profit.

On the other hand, the Feds might have located the ship after Tnaryt's cruiser took off. With the hatch open, they may have spotted the gap in the unrelenting sand. And hauled Isin out when they'd found him on the stairs.

He could be dead from complications related to his injury. Or rotting in a jail cell somewhere. He would have had a difficult time explaining his presence without implicating himself as a smuggler, no matter how good a negotiator he was.

At least the Setarips had taken *Gypsy* and the load of contraband with them.

She turned to Marlin. "He isn't here."

He stood by the railing, watching her. "So I see." His mouth remained frozen in a frown. "But neither were any of the dead crewmembers you mentioned."

"I know." And that pretty much ruled out Mirko as Isin's savior. She wouldn't have removed the dead. Or sealed the hatch. But Feds would.

They hadn't touched anything else, though. If they had any plans to salvage the ship, they would have done it already. Instead, they'd sealed it away and left it to the dunes, like closing off the entrance to an abandoned mine. Which indicated they weren't coming back.

Good news for her. Bad news for Isin.

She stared at the dried blood splotches. Whether he was dead or alive, there wasn't a damn thing she could do to help him now. She'd made her sacrifice. Maybe he'd found his own way to freedom. Or maybe he was buried with the rest of the crew from this ship. Either way, she needed to close that chapter of her life and focus on the future, not the past. She'd already wasted enough time chasing ghosts.

And she had a ship to repair. Pulling back her shoulders, she faced Marlin. "Let's get to work."

Four

Marlin remained glued to her side as they worked their way through the ship. They didn't find any bodies, but they did have to dodge a lot of debris. The passenger staterooms on B deck were a jumbled mess, with items from the countertops and bookshelves tossed on the floor beside the mattresses and bedding.

C deck looked haggard, although most of the furnishings in the dining room and other social areas were still attached to the deck and bulkheads. Panels had popped off during the crash, while smashed bits of earthenware, glass, and tech littered the deck, creating an obstacle course. The galley had taken a hit, with many of the pots, pans, and cooking utensils flung from their storage containers and bins. Whatever food had been onboard had long since shriveled to dust in the dry air. Marlin had grumbled plenty about the amount of work it would take to get the refrigeration units and pantry in serviceable condition after they restored power.

The crew cabins on A deck had survived with minimal damage. They had sparser furnishings and most items had been secured.

She and Marlin had taken a cursory look at the small bridge before heading down to D deck to assess the damage to the ship's main systems. She'd focused on the engine room while he'd checked the water tanks and plumbing.

Cataloging the extensive damage to the engines and electrical systems had given her a lot of clues as to the cause of the crash. The evidence indicated the ship had suffered a mechanical malfunction rather than an attack. The problem had originated in the engine room, triggering an electrical surge and cascade failure that had fried most of the ship's systems.

A maintenance log contained a repair order from Sage dated eleven years earlier. It described the very part that had failed in flight. Either the replacement part had been faulty, or it had been improperly installed. The ship probably hadn't even made it out of atmo. The comm system had been affected by the overload, so the crew wouldn't have been able to call for help, either.

However, that didn't explain why the crew had died. The pilot had successfully landed the ship in the dunes without causing any structural damage to the hull, so someone should have survived. And yet, that didn't appear to be the case. The only logical explanation was that the engine failure had corrupted the life support system, pumping toxins into the atmosphere, and asphyxiating the crew. If that were true, the carcinogens had dissipated long ago. The sensors on her comband weren't picking up any signs of dangerous contaminants.

She backed out of the crawlspace in the engine room and brushed her hands on her pants. "You're definitely a fixer-upper." And much as she hated to admit it, she might be in over her head. She'd maintained engines before, and had learned a lot out of necessity while with the Setarips, but the amount of work needed here intimidated her. She could remove the damaged parts and purchase replacements, but a lot of the connections were demolished beyond recognition. She wasn't convinced she could figure it out without a guide. And if she hooked them up incorrectly, she could kill herself. Or cause another crash. She didn't like either option.

Of course, she could always hire an engineer—there were plenty to be found in Sage—but she didn't have cash on hand. And there was also the risk that anyone she hired might try to take the ship from her. Or report her to the Feds.

She rubbed her hand over her forehead to relieve the tension building there. Maybe she should take a break.

She left the engine room, making her way to the compartment that housed the ship's water tanks.

The glow from her comband swept over the large cylinders, but she didn't see Marlin anywhere. "Marlin?"

"Over here." He came around the curve of one of the drums. "You'll be happy to hear the tanks are sound. I haven't determined yet if the water inside can be made potable."

"What about the filtration system?"

"It's burned out. I'm assuming it can be rebuilt, but I can't do it."

"I might be able to." And if not, she'd add that item to the wish list for her hypothetical engineer.

"Thought so." He gestured to the tanks. "I've checked the main plumbing lines, and other than a few broken joints, they seem to be in decent shape. Fixing the joints should only take a day or two. Of course I won't be able to check the entire system until the console is repaired and we can pump water through the pipes."

"And to do that, we'll need power." She was beginning to understand just how big a job she'd set for herself. "Keep a list of what you anticipate you'll need. We'll search the ship for spare parts first, then make a run to Sage to pick up whatever we can't find here."

Five

Two nights of crawling around the ship had left Nat exhausted but happy. They'd located more spare parts onboard than she'd anticipated, which would help keep their repair costs down. But the larger components would still be pricey. Hopefully she'd make enough selling the non-food items Tnaryt had left in *Gypsy*'s cargo hold that she'd be able to pay for what they needed to get started.

They'd returned to their base camp well before sunrise, taking turns getting some shuteye. They had a big day today, and she wanted to be alert. The shops in Sage would be opening soon, and she wanted to slip in during the hustle and bustle of the morning so they could get lost in the crowd.

The early morning sun filtered through *Gypsy*'s viewport, highlighting dust particles dancing in the air in front of her. She scrolled through the list on her comband display, confirming she'd noted everything they needed, then pushed out of the pilot's seat and strode to the cargo area where Marlin was curled up on his bunk, snoring like a pup.

"Marlin?" No response. She gave his shoulder a shake.

He snapped awake with a full body jerk, the back of his hand striking the bulkhead. He yelped and clasped the injured hand in his palm before glaring at her.

"Sorry. Didn't mean to startle you." She fetched the med kit, rifling through the contents until she located the jar of arnica cream. "Here. Rub that in. It will help."

He took the jar with an annoyed grunt and pulled off the lid. "How long was I asleep?" he asked with a yawn.

"A couple hours."

"Felt like a couple minutes." He stood, stretching his arms over his head. "I'll make us something to eat before we head to Sage."

"I could just grab something from the crates." She was too excited to have much of an appetite.

"No, no." He ran his fingers through his thinning mop of curly hair. "Best to start off with a hot meal."

They were in the air forty minutes later, leaving the mountains behind as they made the cross-country journey.

"What's Sage like?" Marlin took a bite from one of the orange wedges in his hand. Unlike her, his appetite hadn't dimmed. He'd snagged the fruit to eat on the way despite having already consumed a hearty breakfast. Juice dribbled down his chin and onto the cleaning rag he'd tucked into the collar of his tunic like a bib.

"Like?" She'd never had to describe Sage to anyone before. "I dunno. It's a... town."

"Anything like Gallows Edge?"

She shuddered. "No, nothing like Gallows Edge." The former mining outpost still featured prominently in her nightmares. "Sage is... industrial-rustic, I guess you'd say. Lots of single-story buildings and hangars, but with trees scattered around and dirt pathways, too. Kind of a cross between a frontier town and a modern shipyard."

Marlin paused with his hand midway to his mouth. "Frontier? Is it lawless?"

Nat snorted. "Hardly. The Feds keep a close eye on everything in town. And even if they didn't, the main industry is starship repair and maintenance. You'll find ships, shuttles, engineers, and mechanics in abundance, but not outlaws."

"But you've been there."

She lifted a brow. "Are you implying I'm an outlaw?"

He shrugged. "You *are* a thief."

"When I have to be. But not when I'm in a place like Sage. That town's too valuable a resource for parts and labor to risk running crosswise with the Feds."

"That's good to hear." He popped another orange slice in his mouth and gazed at the passing landscape.

She studied him out of the corner of her eye. Originally she'd thought his skittish behavior was something he'd developed as a result of the trauma he'd endured during his captivity with Tnaryt. But she was beginning to suspect it was a personality trait he'd had all his life. If she was right, she'd need to keep that in mind. If they came under fire, he was likely to be even less help to her than Isin had been.

Isin. She'd struggled to put him out of her mind during the past two days, without much success. Guilt pulled at her. Ridiculous, of course, since she'd risked her life to save him. If the end result wasn't what she'd hoped, that wasn't her fault. But still...

She sighed. *Focus on the present, not the past.*

Simple to say. Harder to do.

As they approached Sage, the trees grew taller and leafier, especially along the river that wound past the mountains and curved around the town's western border.

Gypsy's comm chimed with an incoming hail. Nat opened the channel.

"This is Sage tower. Please identify yourself."

"This is cargo shuttle *Gypsy*, requesting permission to land in the prairie lot."

"Please transmit your identification codes."

"Transmitting." She sent the requested data. *Gypsy* had never been tagged by the Galactic Fleet or local authorities for illegal activity, so her IDs were clean. Well, except at Gallows Edge, but that was a very different situation. No one there would be sharing information with the Feds or the Fleet.

"Codes received. What is the purpose of your visit?"

"Commerce."

"How long will you be staying?"

"Just for today."

"One moment, please."

Nat tapped out a rhythm on the controls with her thumb while she waited.

"Cargo shuttle *Gypsy*, you may proceed to the prairie lot following your current trajectory. Please be advised that you accept full responsibility for the safety of your ship and crew by docking in a non-secured area."

"Understood."

She circled the perimeter of the town, bypassing the fenced shipyards and hangars to the north and heading for the open ground to the east.

"Non-secured area?"

She glanced at Marlin. "Docking costs money. Prairie parking is free."

His brow furrowed. "Is it safe?"

She bit her cheek to keep from sighing. "Yes. It's perfectly safe."

She settled *Gypsy* next to a cargo freighter that had seen better days. At least, that's what the exterior said. She'd been around enough ships to know a rough-and-tumble hull often hid a well-maintained interior. Sometimes it paid to be underestimated. Especially when carrying contraband.

Not that they were likely to encounter any illegal activities in Sage. She'd told Marlin the truth. The town was the best place for parts and repairs in the sector, and the

Feds kept a close eye on all transactions. Getting blacklisted here could put a crew out of business. Those looking to provide smuggling services might occasionally strike a deal in one of the town's taverns, but any exchanges of goods or services would take place far from Sage's borders.

Marlin followed her into the cargo hold. "It looks like a long walk into town. How are we going to haul the items to sell?"

"I have a cargo dolly. We'll be fine."

She crouched in the middle of the aisle and slid the deck plating aside, raising the dolly out of a storage compartment and setting it on hover mode before moving the plating back into place.

Marlin seemed suitably impressed. "Handy."

"Yes, it is."

He helped her load six of the crates onto the dolly. He puffed a bit from the effort, but then again he hadn't spent most of his life hauling cargo.

She had.

"Where to first?" he asked, following her as she pushed the dolly down the ramp.

She paused to close the back hatch. "The Armory. The weapons will bring the best price." And they were the items she wanted out of her sight as soon as possible. She couldn't look at them without remembering the fate of their former owners, the people she'd kidnapped and delivered to Tnaryt to save her own skin.

The dirt of the prairie lot gave way to a marked pathway as they reached the edge of town and joined the steady flow of people.

"Busy place," Marlin commented, sidestepping to avoid colliding with a woman carrying three large boxes that hid the lower half of her face. He bumped into the dolly instead, banging his elbow on one of the crates. "Ow."

Nat shook her head. Marlin was proving to be accident-prone. She might need to stock up on the arnica cream. And everything else in the med kit.

"Stay to the left," she instructed, guiding the dolly down a slope as the pathway branched. The buildings lining this section of town were mostly merchandise shops offering clothing, dried goods, and firearms. She halted in front of a shop with an array of rifles and handguns displayed in the window. A sign above the door said *The Armory* in bold script.

Nat lowered the dolly to the ground and set the locking mechanism to keep anyone from moving it or tampering with the cargo. Taking a deep breath, she pushed open the door.

A bell chimed and the shop owner looked up from her post behind the counter.

"Hi, Dane."

Dane's round face split into a grin. "Orlov! Haven't seen you in a coon's age, girl. Where you been?"

Nat returned the smile. She hadn't received a greeting like that since... well, the last time she was in Dane's shop. "Here and there. How are you?"

"Happy as a pig in a puddle. You carryin' your Reiter?"

Nat slid the pistol out of the custom holster she'd sewn into the interior of her duster. "Always."

Dane nodded in approval. "That's one of the prettiest handguns I've ever had come through this place."

And Dane had held onto it for two years until Nat had earned enough to pay for it. She was particular about who bought her merchandise. If she didn't like someone, no amount of money would convince her to part with so much as a paring knife.

"Who's your friend?" Dane gestured to Marlin.

"Marlin Brooks. He's my business partner."

"Business partner, huh?" Dane shot Nat a sidelong glance before sticking out her hand. "Pleased to meet you, Brooks."

Marlin looked like a cat trapped in a room full of rocking chairs as his gaze darted from Dane to the racks of rifles displayed behind her. He slowly extended his hand. "Hi."

She grasped it in hers and gave it a hearty shake, making him sway like a sapling caught in a stiff wind. Dane often had that effect on people. She was a force of nature.

She released him and turned to Nat. "So, you're not with Mirko anymore?"

Those days felt like a lifetime ago. "Not for a year."

"Good riddance, I say. You deserved far better than the way that woman treated you."

Nat grimaced. She hadn't exactly left Mirko by choice. "Have you seen her recently? Or any of the other crew?" Isin had never set foot in Dane's shop—he didn't care for weapons—but some of the other crewmembers from the *Sphinx* might have been in. And shared news of his fate.

Dane shook her head. "Can't say I have. Not since the last time I saw you. You know well as me that Mirko and I never saw eye to eye. Specially when it came to you. She wouldn't walk through my door even if you paid her. I suspect she told most of her crew to steer clear, too. But you never listened." Dane smiled. "You lookin' for her?"

"No. Just curious." And she didn't want to explain why she was asking, either. No reason to drag Dane into the quagmire.

Dane glanced out the window. "Judgin' by the crates on that dolly, you didn't come here for a social call. You got merchandise for me?"

Nat nodded. "Salvaged items."

"Then let's see what you got."

Marlin backed up to the wall to let them pass, and then held the door while Nat and Dane grabbed the crates off the dolly and carried them to the counter.

Dane's eyes lit up as she sorted through the contents. "These'll turn a good profit. What you want for the lot?"

"Whatever you think's fair." She wasn't about to haggle. Dane was a straight shooter, a trait that in her experience was in rare supply. Besides, negotiating tended to give her a headache. She'd never understood why some people enjoyed it. Isin, for one. He'd thrived on it.

Dane shook her head. "Girl, you ain't never gonna make it in this universe if you keep takin' whatever you're given. Wait here." She disappeared into the back room, returning a few moments later with a handful of credit squares. She slid each one across the scanner so the total showed on the display facing Nat.

Nat's jaw dropped. "Dane! That's too—"

"No, it ain't! Now you take this and don't say another word. You're runnin' a new business. Put this to good use."

Her throat tightened, but she wasn't an idiot. She pocketed the squares. "Thank you."

"You can thank me with a nice drink and a good story after you turn that money into somethin' special."

"Deal."

"Now git. Brooks, it surely was a pleasure meetin' you."

"Uh, yeah. You, too." Marlin followed Nat out. He hadn't said a word while they were inside, but he piped up the minute the door closed behind them. "I thought you said you didn't have any friends."

"I don't."

His harrumph made her glance over. He was staring at her with an odd smile on his face.

"What?"

He shook his head. "I just can't wait to meet your next non-friend."

Six

Nat took a sip from the chilled mug in her hand, savoring the earthy taste of the brew. It almost seemed a shame to swallow it. But she did. She was celebrating, after all.

Thanks to Dane's generosity, she'd had enough to purchase every item on her regular list, as well as a few things from her wish list, including a replacement navigation unit. She'd expected to have to shuttle freight for weeks before she'd be able to afford it. Some of the components were secondhand, but that was okay with her. All the ships she'd worked on had been older models with well-worn parts. Those were the ones she could trust to hold together.

It also meant she wouldn't have to make another run to Sage anytime soon. The less attention they drew to their presence on Troi, the better. She didn't want the tower control to start asking questions about where she was coming from and where she was headed.

Marlin had helped her load all the equipment in *Gypsy*'s hold, a bit of a tight fit. Afterward, she'd chosen to enjoy a pint in one of the taverns while he'd headed to the market to pick out some herbs and spices. Since she was reaping the benefits of his cooking, if he wanted to spend a little of their cash on flavorings, she wasn't going to stop him.

She lifted the mug to her lips. The second pull tasted even better than the first. She hadn't factored in the pleasure of enjoying a beer without a collar fastened around her neck that would kill her if she dawdled too long. And she no longer smelled like a walking sewer, either.

For the first time since the Setarip cruiser had knocked *Gypsy* out of the sky, she felt completely human again. At the bar on Gallows Edge, she'd been a pariah to everyone except Doohan, the bartender. Here, no one stared, no one avoided her. She was blissfully ordinary.

"Can I get a whiskey, neat?"

She turned.

The man who'd spoken sat four stools down. He swiped a work cap off his head and tossed it on the bar. *Vitana* was emblazoned across the front in bold black letters outlined in red.

She recognized the name. The engineering installation and repair company was the largest in Sage. More ships went in and out of their hangars in a day than most places saw in a week.

The bartender, a young woman about Nat's age, set the glass of whiskey in front of him. "Rough day, Pete?"

"Last day."

She cocked her head. "What do you mean?"

"I quit."

"You quit? Why?"

He drained the glass in one swallow before answering. "Couldn't take it no more."

A frown line appeared between the bartender's neatly shaped brows. She leaned her forearms on the counter. "But they're your family. Surely you can talk to—"

"Nope. Done talkin'. Done with the lyin', the cheatin', the empty promises. Nothin' ever changes." He tapped his finger next to the empty glass. "Hit me again."

The bartender pursed her lips, but she fetched his drink. "What will you do for work?"

"Don't know. Don't care." The second drink disappeared as quickly as the first, followed by another tap on the bar.

Nat returned her attention to her own drink, not wanting to get caught staring. But that didn't mean she stopped listening.

"You gotta have a job, Pete." The third glass thunked on the bar with a little more force than the previous two.

"No, I don't. I own my place free and clear and got money socked away. I'm good."

Nat watched him out of the corner of her eye. This time he sipped from the glass rather than chugging it, his mouth turned down in a scowl.

The bartender shook her head. "If you say so." She moved off to take care of another customer.

He set the glass on the bar, turning it in his hands as he gazed into its depths. The expression on his face conveyed an emptiness Nat recognized all too well. Not long ago, that had been her.

Taking her drink in hand, she slid off her stool and approached him. This early in the afternoon the place was mostly deserted, so the stools on either side of him were empty. "Mind if I join you?"

He glanced up, apparently surprised to find someone there. For a moment the emptiness receded, but the flicker of life died quickly. He shook his head. "I wouldn't be good company."

"That's okay." She slid onto the stool to his left. "I'm usually not, either."

He frowned, though he looked more confused than upset.

This close, she could see the lines that spread out from his eyes and along his cheeks. She'd put his age at nearly twice hers, though if he'd lived most of his life on Troi, his skin could be weathered by the elements, making him look older. She didn't see any grey in his hair, but the ginger color indicated he was a natural redhead. She'd heard they didn't tend to go grey.

She set down her drink and stuck out her hand. "I'm Nat."

He eyed her warily, emphasizing all those lines. "Look, I don't wanna be rude—I mean, you're pretty and all— but I ain't interested in payin' for sex."

His blunt assumption startled a bark of laughter from her lips. The thought hadn't even occurred to her. He was old enough to be her father. Hell, for all she knew, he *was* her father. She'd never met the man. "I'm a pilot."

A flush crept into his cheeks, visible even through his scruffy beard. "Sorry," he mumbled, returning his gaze to his drink.

"Don't be. I'm flattered." No one had ever mistaken her for a prostitute before. Her boyish figure didn't draw that kind of attention.

He glanced at her, but the flush remained. "Then why do you wanna talk to me?"

She nodded toward his cap. "Are you an engineer?"

"Yep."

"Any good?"

Twin lines grooved his forehead and the wariness returned. "Why you wanna know?"

"I'm looking for an engineer. A good one." And he might fit the bill. Her time with Tnaryt had honed her skills at reading people. She'd bet everything in *Gypsy*'s hold that she was sitting next to a diamond in the rough.

He shook his head, his shoulders drooping. "Don't need a job. Thanks anyway."

She rested her elbow on the bar and leaned a little closer. "You sure? I don't know about you, but sitting around with nothing to do all day doesn't sound like fun. I'd rather have a challenge, working with folks who'd appreciate my talents." Not that she'd ever experienced that with any of her previous employers. And certainly not with Tnaryt. But on her own ship, she could create it.

He met her gaze. "Why would you hire me? You don't know me."

She bit back a smile. He was actually trying to talk her *out* of hiring him. "I'm an excellent judge of character. And I don't like seeing good folks beaten down by bad ones."

He shook his head. "They're not bad. They're just... well... they're just..."

"Family?"

The hint of a smile touched his lips. "Yeah. Family."

She nodded. "Working with family can be tough." She didn't have any experience with that, either. Her mom had died when she was a kid. But she'd seen family dynamics play out with her crewmates often enough to understand the potential landmines.

"Yeah."

"Maybe it's time for something new."

He gazed at her for a long moment, the wheels clearly turning. "What do you need an engineer for?"

"Repairing and maintaining a starship." And with his skillset added to hers and Marlin's, they'd probably be able to finish the job in a respectable timeframe. Months, rather than years.

"Plenty of folks here who can do that."

"I'm not talking about here on Troi. I'm looking for someone to join my crew."

His eyes widened. "You mean, like livin' on the ship? Permanent?"

She nodded. "You'd have an equal share in all profits, your own cabin, and free run of the ship." At least he would when they got it out of the sand.

"An *equal* share?" He said it like the concept was completely foreign.

"As long as you keep the ship in good working order."

He sat up straighter. "I sign on for a job, I get it done."

"I believe you." He'd taken the bait. All she needed to do was reel him in. "And no problem traveling? We might not make it back to Troi very often. You said you have a place here."

"Yeah, I do, but..." He rubbed his hand over his beard. "What did you say your name was again?"

"Natasha Orlov. Call me Nat." The bartender had called him Pete, so she figured he'd appreciate the informality.

"I'm Pete. Pete Stevens."

"Pleased to meet you, Pete."

His head dipped in a small nod. "So, are you the captain of your ship?"

"Yep. And the pilot. It's a small crew."

"How many others?"

"Just one."

His brows lifted, his face growing more animated with each passing moment. "How soon would I start?"

"As soon as you can. Today, if you can swing it."

"Today?"

She nodded. "The ship needs work, and I want to finish it as quickly as possible." Understatement of the galaxy.

"Today," he echoed, his gaze darting to the door and back to her.

"I know it's sudden. If you need a few days to think about it—"

"I'm in."

She squelched the grin that pulled at her lips. "You're sure?"

"Yeah, I'm sure." He picked up the cap and jammed it onto his head. "Just tell me which hangar you're in and—"

"No hangar. The ship's not in town. My partner and I came here in our shuttle."

"Oh. Okay." He stood. "I need to run home and throw some things in a case. How soon you leavin'?"

She checked the chronometer on her comband. They still had a few hours until sunset. "Is an hour enough time to get what you need?"

"Sure."

"Then meet me at the shuttle. *Gypsy*. Prairie lot. One hour."

Seven

Marlin was sorting containers in the cupboards above the compact stove when Nat returned to *Gypsy*. Small packets of herbs and spices overflowed from the box perched on the crates behind him.

He turned as she stopped beside him. "You're looking... chipper. Did you have fun at the bar?"

"Sure did. I met someone."

"Did you?" He crossed his arms in a pose that made him look like a concerned parent. "Who?"

"Pete Stevens. He's an engineer. A good one. He's going to join our crew."

The concern shifted to alarm. He glanced over her shoulder, like he expected to find Pete trussed up on the ground behind her. "Where is he?"

She fisted her hands on her hips. "Relax, Marlin. I didn't kidnap him. He'll be along shortly. He has a place in town and wanted to pick up some things before joining us."

"And no pistols were involved in his decision-making?"

Her good humor seeped away. "No." She deserved his skepticism. She'd earned it the hard way. But it still hurt. "I told you, I'm done with that."

He studied her for a moment before going back to sorting the spices. "Just checking."

She wanted to defend herself, but what more could she say? After what she'd put him through, earning his trust would take time.

She retreated to the cockpit and sank into the pilot's chair, ignoring the dull ache in her chest. Eventually Marlin's suspicion would fade. Maybe having Pete with them would help.

After entering the nav information for their return journey, she pulled up the images she'd taken of the engine room during her inspection. She had a rough plan sketched out for the tasks she wanted to complete, but adding Pete to the equation changed the timetable. She might even be able to start work on the bridge.

She was deep into revising and assigning tasks when *Gypsy's* hatch comm buzzed. She switched on the exterior camera. Pete stood outside, bouncing slightly on the balls of his feet, a large satchel over his shoulder and his long hair pulled back in a neat ponytail. He'd shaved. And ditched his *Vitana* cap.

She touched the comm. "Be right there, Pete." Clearing the images from *Gypsy's* display, she sent the command to open the back hatch and headed to the cargo area.

Marlin had finished organizing the spices and had positioned himself slightly behind the nearest stack of crates, his gaze on the back hatch.

She shot him a glance. "Hiding?"

"Showing caution."

"We need to work on your trust issues," she called over her shoulder, continuing to the hatch. Not that she was one to talk.

Pete had one foot on the ramp, but the uncertainty she'd seen in the bar had returned. He straightened when he saw her. "Hey, Nat."

"Hey, Pete. Come on in." She motioned him forward, which got him past the threshold. He seemed almost as

skittish as Marlin, though in a different way. He looked like
he was waiting for someone to boot him back out.

"Pete Stevens, I'd like you to meet our cook and
part-time plumber, Marlin Brooks."

Marlin had taken a step into the aisle, so at least he
was visible, but his lack of enthusiasm was evident.

Pete's head bobbed in something that was part nod,
part bow. "Pleased to meet ya', Mr. Brooks."

They were probably about the same age, but the
deference in Pete's voice seemed to create a crack in
Marlin's reserve. "Call me Marlin." He stuck out his hand and
Pete shook it. "I hear you're an engineer."

"Yep. It's all I know."

The crack widened. "Well, we can certainly use a
man with your talents on this job."

"I aim to help any way I can."

Nat almost chuckled at the small smile that
appeared on Marlin's face. Pete was winning him over.

She cleared her throat. "If you'll help Pete get his
gear stowed, I'll get us in the air."

"Fine. What kind of food do you like, Pete?"

"I'm not particular, but I got a weakness for anythin'
with curry."

"You're in luck. I just picked some up."

She left the pair to their discussion, shaking her
head as she settled into the pilot's seat. "*Gypsy*, if I live to a
hundred and fifty, I will never understand what makes men
tick."

Eight

"I forgot to ask. What model ship you flyin'?"

Nat glanced at Pete as he dropped into the co-pilot's seat. They were less than ten minutes from their destination, so she was scanning for any other vessels in the area. She'd already made sure no one had followed them from Sage.

"It's a former passenger freighter."

He gazed out at the sea of sand. "And it's docked out here?"

"That's right."

He frowned. "Why? If it needs repairin', wouldn't you want it close to Sage?"

"Well..." She'd already rehearsed what she was going to say. Of course, he might demand she take him back to Sage after she told him the whole truth, but she doubted it. He had an explorer's soul. She met his gaze. "This is where I found it."

"Found it?"

"That's right. Buried in the sand. It's been there for years, untouched. I want to repair it, get it back in the air."

The wariness he'd shown previously returned. "So you ain't the owner?"

"Officially? No. I stumbled onto it a year ago. It was clear I was the first person who'd been onboard since it had crashed. No one ever came looking for it, or if they did, they didn't find it. It's been abandoned."

Some of the tension left his face. "So it's salvage?"

"That's right."

"And you're restorin' it?"

"Exactly. It's a beautiful ship. And from what I can see, structurally sound. The majority of the damage is to the engines and electrical systems."

"So you fix it up and get it flyin'. Then what?"

"We'll live on it. Use it to haul freight. And maybe a few passengers." She hadn't made any decisions on that point yet.

"How much work does it need?"

"I'm hoping you can help me answer that question. I have some engineering experience, but I've never tackled something this big before."

He rubbed his chin. It looked like a nervous habit. "And it's just you and Marlin workin' on it?"

"And you. Assuming you still want the job."

He didn't answer her, just stared out the viewport as she guided *Gypsy* over the sand. The sun had already dipped below the horizon, but enough light remained to outline the dune that covered the ship.

Nat pointed it out. "That's the one."

Pete leaned forward. "Huh."

A quick glance at his face told her she'd snagged his curiosity. He was staring at the dune with rapt attention.

She settled *Gypsy* onto the sand in the valley between two dunes. Slipping off her duster, she hung it on the peg behind the pilot's seat before motioning to Pete to follow her. "Come on. I'll give you a tour."

Marlin had already lifted the cargo dolly out of the storage compartment.

She snagged one of the crates of equipment they'd purchased and set it on the dolly. "We'll take the lighter items on this first trip," she told Marlin. "You and I can come back for the heavier ones while Pete's familiarizing himself with the engines."

"Okay."

Pete insisted on helping them load the dolly and secure the bindings to keep anything from shifting in transit as they climbed the dune.

Nat opened the back hatch and eased the dolly down the ramp to the sand.

Climbing the dune with the dolly took more effort than navigating through the streets of Sage, mostly because her boots kept sinking into the sand, throwing off her balance. When she noticed Pete was plowing up the dunes like a Siberian Husky through snow, she turned the task of steering over to him while she and Marlin walked on either side of the dolly, directing him toward the hatch.

The wind had obviously blown steadily for much of the day, depositing more sand, but with three sets of hands, they cleared the hatch in record time. Marlin and Pete went down first, while Nat stayed above to hand down the crates. After the last crate was unloaded, she joined them below.

Pete brushed his hands together as his gaze swept the darkness of the A deck corridor. "Any power?"

"Not yet." She panned the light for her comband in the opposite direction from Marlin's. "The engine malfunction fried most of the electrical connections. We've positioned a few lanterns where we'll be working."

"Which way to the engine room?"

"Down there." She pointed to the aft. "But if you'd like to see the rest of the ship fir–"

"Just the engines. That's why I'm here."

And he looked eager to get started. Apparently the prospect of this adventure was working its magic on him, too. Good news for her. "Then grab a crate and follow me."

Nine

Twenty minutes later, Pete was happily ensconced in the engine room and Nat and Marlin were back on A deck.

"He's... focused."

Nat couldn't tell from Marlin's tone whether he thought that was good or bad. "Yep. He might be able to finish the repairs in half the time I'd projected."

"Unless he uncovers a bigger problem than you thought."

"Or discovers it's even simpler to fix than I imagined," she countered.

He sighed.

"Come on, Marlin. Show some optimism."

"You be optimistic. I'll be realistic."

She shook her head. He could be right, of course, but meeting Pete had been a stroke of good fortune. She wanted to see that trend continue.

She climbed the ladder to the outer hatch and stepped onto the sand. After freeing the cargo dolly from the anchors, she and Marlin started down the dune, using the dolly as counterweight to manage their descent. *Gypsy's* familiar outline materialized out of the darkness as the light from their combands reflected off the hull in cadence with their steps.

When they reached the bottom, she turned to Marlin. "We'll—"

His eyes widened, staring at a point over her shoulder.

Reacting on instinct, she released the dolly, her hand dropping to her holster as she crouched and pivoted.

A dark shadow moved at the edge of her comband light.

Marlin squealed like a piglet, the sound instantly muffled.

Nat spun toward him, but an arm snaked around her neck and yanked her against the hard planes of an armored torso. A hand clamped over her nose and mouth, cutting off her air, while her captor's other arm pinned her shooting hand to her side.

She struggled, the light from her comband splashing over Marlin, who was caged in by a figure dressed all in black with arms the size of tree trunks.

Nat tossed her head, fighting for air, but the hand over her face clamped down harder, the arm around her torso compressing her ribcage. Changing tactics, she slammed her head back, making contact.

A decidedly female grunt was followed by intense pressure that twisted Nat's head toward her shoulder.

"Want me to snap your neck?" the woman's voice hissed in her ear.

Nat stilled. Judging by the strength in the woman's grip, she could do it.

A third figure materialized out of the shadows, definitely male and almost as large as the man holding Marlin. He faced Nat, remaining just outside the half-circle of light from her comband, the ambient glow illuminating his body partway up his chest.

That was plenty. Muscles rippled under the form-fitting fabric covering his arms and legs, highlighting the armor over his torso and the rifle in his hand.

"You're trespassing on my property."

His low growl poked slivers of ice under her skin, promising violence in every syllable. His next words confirmed it.

"You deserve death. But since I'm not in the habit of killing young boys, I'm going to give you and your father a chance to leave before I slit your throats."

Her mind whirled. This man thought she was a boy? And that Marlin was her father? What a joke.

But he'd also just laid claim to *her* ship. And apparently was prepared to kill her for it.

"Why don't you let me have fun with him first?" The grip on Nat's mouth eased as the woman stroked a thumb along her cheek. "He's young. I could break him in."

Her skin crawled at the woman's seductive purr.

"Shut it, Shash. We're not here for your entertainment." The man took a step closer, the light revealing a thick neck and skin almost as dark as the fabric covering his torso. "What's it going to be, boy?"

She forced air into her constricted lungs. She needed to be sensible. Smart. It was only a ship, right? If she died tonight defending it, what would that prove? That she was an idiot?

But her more primitive side refused to listen to logic, sweeping away her fear and replacing it with white-hot anger. It *wasn't* just a ship. It was her future. And what was left of her past. She'd suffered under the thumb of a brute just like this one, enduring untold horrors so she could make it back here. If she gave up now, slinking off into the night, all that agony had been for nothing.

A year of pent-up rage and pain crested, devouring everything in its path. Shifting her weight, she shoved back against the woman holding her. "I'm not a boy, you pea-brained gorilla!" she yelled as she kicked out. her foot connecting solidly with the man's chest.

He didn't move. Not to block the blow, and not in reaction after it landed. She might as well have kicked a marble statue. Her foot certainly throbbed like she had.

The woman. Shash. yanked Nat off her feet and crushed her windpipe in a vicious grip.

Nat strained against the intense pressure. Apparently learning she was a female had ruined her standing in Shash's eyes.

The light from her comband swung wildly. glancing off the shaved head. livid scar. and dark eyes of the man who still stood like carved stone. staring at her in... *shock?*

"Let her go."

His words barely registered. Nat was too busy trying to breathe. She needed air. but the pressure increased. making her vision grey around the edges.

"Are you nuts?" Shash snarled. her fingers remaining locked like steel bands. "She's—"

"*Get your hands off her!*"

The roar echoed in Nat's ears. joining the pounding thump of her pulse as her heart worked to keep blood flowing to her brain. The tension around her throat and body abruptly ceased. She dropped to the sand like a ragdoll. barely catching herself before her face made contact. She sucked in air in rasping gulps. coughing as she inhaled dust and sand at the same time.

When a hand touched her arm. she jerked back. rolling away and staggering into a defensive posture.

"Natasha?"

Her blood froze. holding her body in place.

The man knelt in front of her. She couldn't see his face—her comband was pointed the wrong way. But his voice had changed. Become softer. More cultured.

She knew that voice. Had heard it a thousand times, playing over and over in her head ever since the day she'd saved—

"*Isin?*"

Ten

Nat's mind rebelled. It couldn't be. Isin might have survived, but there was no way this monster could possibly be—

She pivoted her arm so that the glow from her comband touched his face. She flinched. A jagged scar grooved his cheek, marring his dark skin. But it was the look in his eyes that really shook her. She was used to seeing arrogance and bitterness there, but a slight vulnerability, too.

Not anymore. The man staring back at her looked like a cold-blooded killer.

She swallowed. "It's you, isn't it?" She still couldn't believe what her senses were telling her. Elhadj Isin. The man who'd come apart when the Setarips had chased them. The man who abhorred violence. The two images didn't match up. But it was him. She knew it before he said a word.

"Yes." He ran a hand over his head. His *shaved* head. Another change. He reached for her arm.

She jerked away, scrambling back.

He followed her. "I won't hurt you."

She kept moving. "That's not what you said before."

"I didn't know—"

"Who I was?"

"That you were alive."

That halted her in her tracks. He'd thought she was *dead?* How strange. In all the time she'd spent wondering if he'd made it off the ship, she'd never, not even once, considered the possibility that he'd been wondering about her fate, too.

"You *know* her?"

Nat and Isin both turned.

Shash had a gun leveled at Nat's head.

And then she didn't. Isin moved between them in a blur, disarming Shash between one breath and the next. "Don't you *ever* threaten her."

Nat's jaw dropped. He was *defending* her? Against his own people?

Shash's face twisted in a snarl as she made a grab for the gun, but Isin was quicker. He had her in a headlock, her body on the ground and her face pressed into the sand, before Nat could blink.

"Be careful, Shash." The words slid from his lips like liquid mercury. "You're valuable, but not irreplaceable."

Nat took an involuntary step back. She didn't know this man. It certainly wasn't Isin. Well, it *was*, physically. But she was staring at a stranger.

She glanced at Marlin. He was still encased in the grip of his captor. His skin looked pale as moonlight, his eyes wide as his gaze darted from her to the pair on the ground.

Isin released Shash and stood, but didn't relax his guard.

She rose slowly, brushing sand off her cheek. She smirked at Nat. "Well aren't you the lucky one? Didn't know he was poking you."

Wham! The solid crack of Isin's fist connecting with Shash's jaw made Nat jump.

Shash staggered, her hand going to the side of her face as her gaze swung to Isin.

He stalked toward her. "Apparently I didn't make myself clear."

Nat couldn't see Isin's expression, but judging by the fear on Shash's face, she didn't want to.

"I got it." Shash continued to back up, holding her hands in front of her like a shield. "I'm sorry."

Isin stopped his advance, but he still looked like a wall of menace, even from the back. "You *will* show her respect."

Shash stared at the sand between her feet. "Yeah. No problem."

Isin didn't move for several long moments, the coiled power in his muscles reminding Nat of a cobra about to strike. When he turned his gaze on her, she tensed.

"I apologize for the interruption. Where were we?"

Nat folded her arms over her chest to hide the tremors wracking her body. She didn't know how to respond to Isin's volatile behavior. She certainly didn't want him to sense how scared she was. Showing fear wouldn't earn her any points. So she fell back on what she did best. She bluffed. "You were about to tell me why you're here."

His brows lifted. "Was I?"

"Yes. After you let my friend go." She nodded at Marlin, who looked one breath away from a meltdown.

"Who is he?"

"Marlin Brooks."

Isin's gaze challenged her. "Who is he to *you?*"

His tone reminded her of Tnaryt. Arrogant. Demanding. She'd had more than enough of that kind of attitude. She lifted her chin. "None of your business."

He stared at her.

She stared right back. She'd be willing to bet his companions were waiting for him to change his mind about killing her. And he might. She couldn't read him at all. But she'd walked through fire to get here. She wasn't backing down.

His expression changed, losing a little of the hard edge. And triggering a memory.

The image flashed into her mind, overlaying the scene like a holographic projection.

"That's something I like about you, Orlov. You speak your mind."

He'd said that to her the first time she'd seen him smile. The *only* time she'd seen him smile, actually.

He looked over his shoulder at the man holding Marlin. "Let him go, Kenji."

Kenji straightened, confusion etched on his face. "You sure about that, Cap?"

Isin's eyes narrowed.

Kenji's arms dropped to his sides with obvious reluctance.

Apparently they'd been the only thing holding Marlin upright. He toppled to the sand in a heap.

"Marlin!" Nat brushed past Isin to reach him. She sank onto the sand and rolled him onto his back. "Marlin? Say something."

His pallor hadn't improved. In fact, it looked like leeches had drained all the blood out of his body. His eyes rolled, showing mostly white.

She glared at Kenji. "What did you do to him?"

He shrugged. "Nothing." His nonchalant attitude didn't match his rippling muscles and military-style crew cut.

She patted Marlin's cheeks with the back of her hand. "Marlin? Can you hear me?"

A groan rumbled up from his chest, followed by a fluttering of his eyelids.

"Marlin?"

He finally responded, his eyes opening and his gaze focusing on her. "Nat?"

"Yeah, it's me. You okay?"

He frowned, considering the question. "I don't know. What happened? I was–" His gaze settled on Kenji and Isin and his Adam's apple bobbed up and down. "Never mind."

"He fainted," Isin said.

"No thanks to you and your goons."

"Goons?" He stared at her, his expression unreadable. "They're part of the best mercenary outfit in the quadrant."

Mercenaries. That explained the scar. But not his sudden appearance on Troi. A sick feeling settled into her stomach. "Why are you here?"

For a split-second, his attitude shifted, giving her a glimpse of–what? She couldn't say. But then it was gone.

"That's something we need to discuss. *Privately.*"

Privately? What could he possibly have to say that he wouldn't want his companions to overhear?

He gestured up the dune in the direction of the ship's hatch. "We can talk in the–"

Nat stood, planting her feet. "No way. If you want to talk, we'll talk out here." She was having enough trouble holding things together without being back on the ship with him. And she didn't trust his friends not to shoot her in the back at the first opportunity.

Isin pinned her with a look that was both familiar and chilling. He'd stared at her that way whenever they'd started in on one of the heated arguments they'd often had while they'd both been working for Mirko on the *Sphinx.* But the changes to his appearance gave the expression a very different effect.

Still, she refused to back down under his piercing gaze. He'd already dominated the situation physically. She wouldn't lose the battle of wills, too.

"Fine." He turned to Kenji and gestured to Marlin. "Take him to the ship and—"

Nat cut him off. "My engineer's onboard."

Isin turned back to her. "You have an engineer with you?"

She bristled at the surprise in his voice. What did he think she was doing out here? Making sand castles? "He's working on repairs. And he might not react well to the appearance of your... mercenaries." For all she knew, Pete might come unglued like Marlin. But she doubted it. He seemed to fall more on the fight side of the fight or flight scale. She didn't want him to get hurt because of her.

Isin's lips pressed together.

She swept her arm behind her. "We can talk in *Gypsy.*"

Isin's gaze followed the movement of her arm and he blinked, as if seeing the shuttle for the first time. "That's *Gypsy?*"

"Yeah."

Incredibly, he seemed at a loss for words. After a few beats, he managed to get one out. "How?"

"I repaired her. After the Setarips took us onboard the cruiser."

The stunned look spread, making him appear more like the man she remembered. "You've been a *captive?*"

"Until a couple weeks ago."

His gaze held hers—searching, questioning. Finally he broke eye contact and glanced at Kenji. "Keep her friend out here, and make sure nothing happens to him." His gaze flicked to Shash in a silent warning. "Alert me if the engineer shows up."

Kenji nodded. "Understood."

Isin turned to her, gesturing toward *Gypsy*'s back hatch. "Lead the way."

Eleven

She'd lost her mind. It was the only explanation for why she'd suggested they use *Gypsy* for this talk. Standing out in the open next to this version of Isin had been terrifying enough. Enclosed in the cargo area with him was like sharing a closet with a walking nightmare.

The lighting inside the shuttle was far less forgiving than her comband, the scar on his face showing in bright relief. The surprise she'd seen in his eyes earlier had been wiped clean, replaced with the cold detachment that appeared to be his new normal.

What happened to you, Isin? She couldn't begin to imagine what had caused such a drastic transformation, but she couldn't very well ask him without insulting him. Or making him angry. Instead, she focused on the most important question. "What are you doing here?"

"Finding out what *you're* doing here. I assume it involves the ship?"

"Of course it involves the ship." She folded her arms. Too bad her duster was in the cockpit. She felt naked under his gaze. At least he hadn't taken her pistol. He clearly didn't view her as a threat. "Why else would I be here?"

"Why else, indeed." He folded his arms, too, his corded muscles concealing the armor plating covering his chest. "What's your plan?"

"Why do you care?"

"Because your presence complicates things."

"Complicates things? For who?"

"Me."

One of the pieces clicked into place. "You're the one who sealed the hatch, aren't you?"

He nodded.

"Why?"

"To keep out trespassers."

She bristled. "I'm not a trespasser."

"I didn't say you were."

Then what was he saying? She changed tactics. "How did you get off the ship? Did the Feds find you?"

"No. Mirko did. Eventually." His eyes glinted with cold malice. "We... parted ways shortly afterward."

She swallowed. Mirko had left them to fend for themselves when the Setarips had attacked. Isin had clearly taken her abandonment personally. "Did you—" She cleared her throat. "Did you kill her?"

"No." The single syllable sliced like a blade. "But I should have. Next time I see her, I'll correct that mistake."

The chilling certainty in his words made her shiver. The Isin she'd known hadn't been capable of killing anyone, even in self-defense. "When did you become a mercenary?"

"The day I could walk again." He gestured to his leg.

Another memory slammed into her. Shrapnel embedded in his calf, hobbling him as they'd struggled to reach the torpedo room. And the blood trail she'd found leading out of that room and up the aft stairway.

Looking at him now, she couldn't believe he was the same man. He'd always been muscular, but now those muscles had an iron, lethal edge. She wasn't even sure shrapnel could make it through anymore. Pain didn't seem to register, either. She'd kicked him with everything she had, and he hadn't even flinched.

"Why'd you do it?"

He tilted his head. "Do what?"

"Become... this?" She swept her hand to encompass all of him. "You're so... different."

His lips parted, but the gesture wasn't a smile. More like baring his teeth. "You don't approve?"

Approve? She was horrified. "Do you... *enjoy*... working as a mercenary?" She hoped not. He hadn't enjoyed working for Mirko, either, but at least he'd been... human.

"That's irrelevant."

"Irrelevant?"

"Yes."

"Why?"

His gaze drifted toward the back hatch. "It's profitable."

She didn't buy it. Isin wasn't the type to be motivated by greed. That was Mirko's arena. "There are other ways to make money." Ways that wouldn't require slicing up his body and killing his soul. Or killing other people.

"Not like this."

She rested her hands on her hips. "So what do you do with all this money you're making?"

His gaze swung back to her. "I own and operate a ship and crew."

She couldn't very well argue with that. She was working toward the same goal. "So the three of you are guns for hire?"

"It's not just the three of us."

Her heartbeat kicked up a notch. "Where's the rest of your crew?" Waiting behind the dunes to pounce on them?

"Finishing the job I left to come here."

So, not preparing to ambush them. That was good news. And yet– "If you were working, why did you leave to come here?"

He gave her a pointed look. "When you opened the seal, you set off my security alarms."

Oh.

"It took a few days to get here from *Vengeance.*"

"*Vengeance?*"

"My ship."

She wasn't going to ask about the charming name. She nodded in the direction of the dune. "So why did you set security alarms on this ship?"

"Because it's mine."

Her skin prickled. "Yours?"

"Yes."

She stared at him. "Says who?"

"Me."

Tension coiled between her shoulder blades. "It's not yours to take."

His stance shifted, his head coming up like a wolf scenting prey. "Why not?"

"Because it's *mine.*"

Twelve

His lips thinned, the scar pulling across his cheek. "Yours?"

Was there an echo? "Yes, *mine.* I spent a year as a slave to a sadistic Setarip because of *you.*" She pointed a finger at his chest. "The *only* thing that kept me going was thinking about that ship. It's *mine.*"

His eyes looked like polished onyx. "Then we have a problem."

"No, *you* have a problem. I have a ship to restore." And now that she knew he was the one who'd sealed the hatch, she didn't have to worry about the Feds showing up to take the ship from her.

She just had to worry about the glowering male in front of her.

She tried to step past him, but he grabbed her upper arm in a steel grip. Her heartbeat kicked into overdrive as he hauled her back as easily as she'd move an empty crate.

"We're not done."

She considered stomping on his foot, but caught herself. Why bother? It would be like a monkey stepping on an elephant.

Instead, she stared into the black hole of his eyes.

"This Setarip. What did it do to you?"

"Why do you care?"

His scowl deepened. "Did it hurt you?"

"That's what sadists do."

"How?"

"What does it matter?"

"Tell me."

"It's not—"

"*Tell me!*" His grip on her arm tightened.

She flinched. He was going to leave marks.

He immediately eased up. His voice changed, too, returning to the softer tones she remembered. "What did the Setarip do to you, Natasha?"

Natasha. Her name on his lips created a fissure in her emotional wall, allowing a rivulet of pain to seep out. She'd listened to his voice in her head so many times during her captivity. Hearing it now rocketed her back to that place of torment and death. A tremor worked its way up from her toes. She did her best to squelch it. "I wore a shock collar. He triggered it for fun. He enjoyed inflicting pain."

The tendons of his neck tightened. "But you escaped?"

"With help, yes."

"And where is this Setarip now?"

"Dead."

His lips pulled up in a snarl. "That's unfortunate."

Unfortunate? "Why?"

His dark eyes unfocused as if he wasn't really seeing her. "He should have died at my hands. Slowly."

She trembled, his grip keeping her from putting distance between them. She'd seen that look before, a hundred times. On Tnaryt's face.

She'd traded one horror for another.

His fingers burned into her skin like brands. She jerked her arm, trying to break the connection. "Let go."

He released her so quickly she staggered, catching herself on the stack of crates. He reached for her, but she ducked, backing away from him.

He halted, his expression unreadable.

Her heart hammered, trying to push through her ribs. She was cowering, just like she had with Tnaryt. She might not have a collar around her neck anymore, but her body was still a captive of her memories.

They stared at each other, neither moving, neither speaking.

A small sound brushed past her. Was that a sigh?

"I can't give you the ship, Natasha."

Straightening her spine took a supreme effort, but she did it. "It's not yours to give, *Elhadj.*" She used his first name on purpose, netting the desired result. He tensed and lost some of his emotional detachment.

Good. She wanted to remind him that he'd been dependent on her for his survival the last time they were together, a fact he seemed inclined to forget. She'd risked her life to save his, dammit. And now he was acting like he owed her nothing.

He drew in a slow breath, his expression switching to the contemplative look he'd often used during a negotiation. "Perhaps we should consider all our options."

She'd have to tread carefully. He was much better at this than she was. "Meaning what?"

"You want the ship repaired and functional, correct?"

"Or course."

"I assume you were planning to start immediately?"

She nodded.

"And it makes sense to complete the work as quickly as possible?"

The Feds hadn't found the ship, but it would be foolish to push her luck. The longer they were out here—and the more shuttle runs they made—the greater the chance that someone would notice and send a patrol to investigate.

But she didn't want to agree with him. He was maneuvering her toward a particular response, and that made her twitchy. "What's your point?"

"We should work together."

"Work together? Why would I agree to that? You want to take my ship."

His mouth pinched. "I don't want to take anything."

"That's not what you just said."

"I'm reevaluating."

"Well reevaluate this. I don't make deals with mercenaries."

"Why not?"

"They can't be trusted."

"Says the thief."

She glared at him. "I may steal, but I keep my word. Mercenaries don't. They follow the money." And right now, her ship was a valuable asset. Well, it would be after it was repaired.

"And here I thought my worst flaw was bitterness."

Her snappy comeback died in her throat. He remembered? She'd said that right before the Setarips had come knocking on the outer hatch. "I didn't think you'd—"

"Remember?" Something shifted in his eyes. "I remember everything from that day."

"Then you should remember I saved your life. You owe me."

"I know."

At least they agreed on that.

"But I also owe my crew. I promised them this ship."

"So what? You're the captain. They have to follow your orders."

His next words poured ice into her veins. "Clearly you've never worked with mercenaries."

She got the implication. If he didn't produce the ship, his crew might turn on him. And her.

She gritted her teeth. He'd just dropped a new set of challenges in her lap. But he also seemed inclined to defend her. Saving his life had earned her that much. Her first priority was finding out how far his sense of obligation would get her, and if it would extend to Marlin and Pete. "What about my crew?"

"What about them?"

"If we agree to work together, can you guarantee Kenji and Shash won't hurt them?" *Or me?*

"As long as they don't attack us."

"And Shash will follow your orders?" He'd just implied his crew couldn't be trusted.

The steel came back into his eyes. "I'll make sure she does."

Nat shuddered. She had a good idea what would happen to Shash if she stepped out of line.

"And after the ship's repaired? What then?"

He shook his head. "I don't have an answer for that. Yet."

She bit the inside of her cheek. Did she have a better option?

She wanted the ship, but to get it, she needed to repair it first. The work would go faster if she went along with his plan. If she said no, she'd force him to choose between her and his crew. She didn't like her odds in that scenario.

But if she had more time to work on him, to convince him she was right, that might change. And while he scared the stuffing out of her, he'd shown he was still capable of being reasonable. Instead of overpowering and threatening her, he was negotiating a truce.

"All right. We'll work together."

And if he proved to be a mercenary at heart, she'd find a way to sneak the ship out from under him.

Thirteen

Marlin was seated between Kenji and Shash when Nat and Isin exited the shuttle, the glow from his comband trembling slightly. He looked like he wanted to burrow into the sand and disappear.

Kenji stood immediately. "We good, Cap?"

"Fine. We're going to work with Natasha and her crew to restore the ship."

His pronouncement was met with stunned silence.

"We are?" Marlin squeaked like a rabbit caught in the jaws of a wolf.

"We are," Nat confirmed.

Shash's gaze swept Nat up and down. She gave a derisive sniff.

Nat crossed her arms over her chest. She'd never wasted time worrying about how others saw her. In most situations she didn't want to be noticed at all. But Shash's attitude was getting under her skin. Clearly she'd judged Nat and found her... lacking.

Get your head in the game, Orlov. She focused on Marlin. "We need to tell Pete about the change in plans."

He stared at her like she'd lost her mind.

Maybe she had. But she didn't see a better way out of this conundrum. "I'll go and—"

Isin stepped in front of her. "We'll go with you."

She scowled, but in the semi-darkness, he looked even more intimidating than in the bright lights of *Gypsy*'s cargo hold. And a lot less trustworthy. "Suit yourself."

She walked around him, reached down, and helped Marlin to his feet.

He wavered, his gaze darting to the three black-clothed figures. His expression pleaded with her to reconsider, but he held his tongue.

"Let's go." She kept her hand under his elbow as they plowed up the dune. She could sense Isin stalking behind her. Or at least that's how it felt. He hadn't allowed her to put more than an arm's length between them since they'd left the shuttle. Maybe he was protecting her from Shash, but it felt more like surveillance than protection.

She stayed by the hatch while Marlin climbed down the ladder into the ship, then followed him. Isin dropped to the ground beside her without using the ladder, making her jump. She shot him a look of annoyance. What did he think she would do—run and hide?

Kenji and Shash joined them, the corridor shrinking as they stood like a moving bulkhead, watching her.

"Pete's in the engine room." Pivoting, she strode to the aft stairs, Marlin glued to her side and Isin on her heels. Walking had never seemed so complicated. And what was she going to tell Pete? Marlin was petrified but pliant, following her lead. She didn't expect her new engineer to be so passive. He might even decide to decamp, which would play right into Isin's hands.

The thump of five sets of boots on the stairs must have alerted Pete to the change in situation. She caught sight of movement around a corner, followed by a partial silhouette of Pete holding the barrel of a weapon she hadn't even known he'd been carrying.

As she shifted the light in his direction, he targeted Isin. "Let 'em go."

The anger in his words surprised her. As did the authority with which he said them. While Marlin had come apart the moment Isin's crew had shown up, Pete looked ready to take them on single-handedly.

Isin halted, resting a hand on Nat's shoulder to stop her, too. "They're not prisoners. Natasha and I are old... friends."

She snorted. They'd never been friends. Rivals. Adversaries. Combatants. But never friends.

Pete didn't miss her reaction. "Seems the lady disagrees."

"Lady, my foot," Shash muttered.

Pete shifted his aim to target Shash. "You best show some respect, ma'am."

Nat shook off Isin's grip, stepping forward before Shash could reply and start a war. "It's okay, Pete. Isin and I made a deal. They're going to help us repair the ship."

"That so?" He didn't sound remotely convinced.

"He and I used to work together on the *Sphinx*. He was with me when I found this ship." And *she* had been the one to find it. True, *finding it* had involved tripping over the hatch handle, but that was a minor detail.

Pete's gaze moved to Isin. "You the reason she got captured by the Setarips?"

Nat blinked. When had he learned *that* bit of information? He and Marlin must have covered a lot of ground during the shuttle ride.

Isin's voice rumbled past her ear. "Yes."

"She saved your life." Pete indicated Nat with a lift of his chin. "Best you be rememberin' that."

"I think about it every day."

Nat glanced at him, but he kept his attention on Pete. Had he *really* thought about her every day? Or was he just saying that to convince Pete to stand down?

Either way, it worked. Pete slowly lowered the gun. "So you're Isin?"

"Yes. This is Kenji and Shash." Isin indicated his companions.

Pete gave a brief nod before facing Nat. "How'd they find you?"

"Apparently Marlin and I set off Isin's security alarm when we opened the outer hatch. He came to investigate."

Isin stepped to Nat's side. "I wasn't expecting to find Natasha."

Pete studied Isin for a moment before meeting Nat's gaze. "I 'spect not. What's the plan?"

Plan? She didn't have a plan. She was making this up as she went along. And she hadn't bothered to ask Isin how he was going to help them with the repairs. She glanced at him. "Most of the damage is to the engines and electrical system. Pete can give instructions for what needs—"

Shash pushed her way to Isin's other side. "I don't need his instructions." She made a dismissive gesture toward Pete. "Just point me to the engine room."

Nat rested her hands on her hips. "So you can do what? Blow it up?"

"Fix it, you stupid little tra—"

Isin silenced her with a look. Tension crackled between them, but Shash lowered her head, staring at the deck.

Isin gave a long-suffering sigh. "Shash is a skilled engineer. Sometimes she thinks she's the only one. She can *assist* your engineer in whatever way *he* deems helpful." The emphasis he put on his words was clearly a message to Shash to toe the line.

Her lips worked like she was fighting to keep her comments to herself. The hostility in her gaze had risen several notches, too. She glared at Nat as though hoping to burn a hole in her forehead.

Great. Another black mark against her in Shash's register. She didn't want to unleash the woman's vitriol on Pete. "Are you willing to work with her?" she asked him.

He didn't bat an eye. "Sure. There's plenty to do."

And Pete had proven he could watch out for himself. If someone had to work with Shash, he was the best choice. "Then we'll leave you to it."

His slight nod indicated he'd gotten the message loud and clear. He picked up the shuttered lantern sitting by his feet and switched it on before motioning to Shash. "This way."

She followed him at a leisurely pace. The air of hostility left with her.

Isin watched them go before turning to Nat. "What else do you need?"

Her gaze took in the mountain of muscles he and Kenji provided. Might as well put it to good use. "We still have parts and supplies to bring up."

"And after that?"

"Marlin's in charge of the galley, plumbing, and water purification system. I'll be working on the bridge, electrical, and outer hatch repair."

"What about *Gypsy?*"

"What about her?"

"Are you planning to leave her exposed out there while you work?"

"She's not that exposed. The mineral content in the sand makes it virtually impossible to pick up metallic signals on a scanner. And we'll be leaving before dayli–" She broke off. No, they wouldn't be leaving. She couldn't very well take *Gypsy* into the mountains during the day like she'd planned, could she? Not with Isin's crew here. No telling what they might do while she was gone.

Isin was studying her. "Leaving to go where?"

"Nowhere. Never mind." But now she had to come up with a way to hide *Gypsy* without moving her. "What about the ship you came in on? Where is it?"

"Concealed nearby."

"Concealed? How?"

"The hull has interchangeable, sensor-dampening skins to disguise it in various environments."

"Convenient."

"Yes." That speculative look was back in his eyes. "We might be able to create something similar for *Gypsy*. Nothing elegant, but functional enough to disguise her from passing patrols."

She'd consider any option that meant she didn't have to leave him alone on this ship. "I'm open to suggestions."

"Good. We can discuss it while we unload the supplies."

Fourteen

"They're going to kill us."

Nat yanked the sheets off the twin bed in one of the passenger cabins on B deck and moved to the next bed. "No they're not." Otherwise she and Marlin wouldn't be wasting their time gathering linens to camouflage *Gypsy*.

"Of course they are. They're toying with us." Marlin wasn't even pretending to help her.

"Isin wouldn't do that." At least, she hoped he wouldn't. The jury was still out on that one.

"They'll kill us as soon as we're not useful anymore."

Nat froze, a shudder passing through her body. *Useful.* That word triggered a lot of bad memories. "They're not like Tnaryt."

Marlin scoffed. "Could have fooled me. Do you trust Mr. Tall, Dark, and Lethal to play nice?"

Nat rolled the sheets into a ball. "No, I don't trust him."

"Then why did you agree to work with him? Why aren't we leaving? This ship isn't worth our lives."

She reined in her temper. Marlin was back to spreading gloom and doom, but getting angry with him wouldn't help. "If you want to leave, I'll take you to Sage right now. Just say the word."

"But you'd come back here?"

"Yes. Nothing's changed for me. I'm not giving up this ship." She stuffed the sheets into one of the canvas drawstring bags she'd found in the ship's laundry room.

Handing it to Marlin, she stepped through the doorway and continued down the corridor to the next cabin.

He trailed behind her. "If they don't kill us, they'll strand us here. They don't need us."

She gritted her teeth. "I won't let that happen." How, she didn't know. It didn't help that Marlin was repeating the same points she'd made with Isin.

"And you think you can stop them? They're walking arsenals."

"I won't have to stop them." Isin would defend her. Probably. And together they'd figure out a way to appease his crew so she could have this ship. Isin wouldn't abandon her here. Would he?

"You're being naïve."

"And you're being pessimistic."

He sighed. "I just thought our days of dealing with sadistic overlords were behind us."

She started gathering another bundle of sheets. "Isin's not sadistic." At least she hoped that was still true.

"Shash is."

"Yeah, well..." She didn't have an answer for that one.

"And she hates you."

"Tell me something I don't know."

They filled four drawstring bags before climbing the stairs to A deck. Marlin stood at the bottom of the ladder while Nat exited through the outer hatch and knelt on the sand.

"Hand one up." She reached for the bag he pushed into the opening, pulling it out and setting it on the ground beside her. Three more followed.

"Okay. I've got them. You can go start on the plumbing repairs."

The light from her comband illuminated Marlin's upturned face. "Or I could help you cover the shuttle."

She shook her head. "We talked about this. We're not going back to base camp, so you need to get the plumbing working so we'll have drinking water and a functioning bathroom. *Gypsy's* reserves won't last for long."

The skin around his eyes pinched. "Yeah. I know." He shuffled his feet. "If you don't hear from me in the next two hours, come look for my corpse."

"Marlin—"

"Yeah, yeah, I'm going." He disappeared down the corridor.

Her gut twisted. Was she being foolish to send him off alone? What if Kenji or Shash *did* hurt him? Or threatened to, using him as a bargaining chip against her? Would Isin allow that kind of coercion?

She pushed to her feet, glancing down to where *Gypsy's* shape was outlined by several lanterns. Isin's dark form moved around the perimeter.

She swept her gaze across the other dunes in the area, looking for any sign of his ship. No luck. Wherever he'd tucked it, she wouldn't find it easily.

As if he needed *another* advantage.

While she and Marlin had been busy gathering sheets, Isin and Kenji had been burying anchors in the sand around *Gypsy* and attaching guiding lines. Isin seemed to be the only one working now, so Kenji must have already returned to the ship.

She snagged one of the bags. "Heads up!" she called out before tossing the bag over the edge of the dune. It struck the sand and rolled, coming to rest near the bottom. She repeated the process with the other three bags and then started down the slope, her boots sinking in the loose sand.

A slight breeze lifted dust into the air, but nothing like the wind that had pelted her the first time she'd stood on this dune. With any luck, the wind would pick up after they'd finished securing the sheets. The tented material covering *Gypsy* would look more like a naturally occurring dune if it were coated with sand.

Isin reached for two of the bags. "Start knotting the corners of the sheets on the guiding lines."

She bristled at his tone. "Is that an order?"

He turned with exquisite slowness to meet her gaze. He looked like he was contemplating using *her* as an anchor. "Yes. Unless you want your shuttle to end up in a federal compound."

She didn't, but his attitude needed a serious adjustment.

He walked away, leaving her to follow his orders, or not, as he moved around to *Gypsy's* other side.

"Arrogant, overbearing, egomaniac," she muttered as she opened one of the bags and grabbed a sheet.

She followed his instructions, attaching the sheets to the guiding lines, but apparently she was a lot slower than he was. She'd barely finished with one bag by the time he'd made his way around to her side, attaching the sheets to the lines above the anchors and feeding them up so they laced across the shuttle's hull. He moved with the self-assurance of someone who'd done this many times before.

She paused to watch, picking up a few pointers from his technique. "Where did you learn how to do this?"

He glanced at her, his expression unreadable. "You don't want to know."

"Oh."

She'd take his word for it. She hurried to finish, but he still caught up to her, attaching the last few sheets before she could get to them.

At least it was done. And she couldn't argue with the result. Even without a covering of sand, the sheets concealed *Gypsy*'s shape. While the camouflage wouldn't hold up under scrutiny, it would be effective as a visual shield for any aircraft passing overhead.

Isin pointed to where *Gypsy*'s back hatch was hidden under the material. "I staked that section so you can still lower the hatch."

"Good. We'll need that until Marlin and Pete get the plumbing functional." Although she didn't intend to offer Isin and his crew access to *Gypsy*. They could hike out to their concealed ship if they needed creature comforts.

"Are you ready to get to work?"

She frowned. "I *have* been working."

"Work on the ship."

Was he trying to pick a fight with her? Or was she just irritable? Either way, her ruff was up. "Not if you're going to order me around."

He took a step closer, the light from the lanterns reflecting in his dark eyes, making them glow. "You sure about that?"

Okay, still terrifying. But she held her ground. "Yes."

He didn't move, but his expression softened a fraction. "You look tired."

The comment caught her off guard. "What's that supposed to mean?"

"It means you look tired. How long have you been up?"

"None of your—"

"Forget it." He held up a hand. "I was just making an observation. You look like you could use some sleep."

She eyed him warily. "So?"

"So maybe you should take a break."

"I bet you'd like that, wouldn't you? Leave you alone to—"

"To what, Natasha?" Anger crept into his voice. "What exactly do you think I'd do?"

"I don't know. That's the point." She fisted her hands on her hips. "And what about you? Do you still sleep? Or did you give that up along with everything else?" The comment came out with a bite.

The tendons in his jaw flexed. "Yes, I sleep."

"Good. Why don't *you* go take a nap?"

He stared at her for a long moment. "I have a better idea. Why don't you show me your plans for the electrical repairs."

"But you don't know anything about electrical." Or anything else having to do with keeping a ship running.

"I do now."

"Oh." So in addition to becoming a mercenary, he'd also picked up practical skills. That was... good?

"Fine. We'll work on the electrical."

"And then we'll take a break for a few hours."

"*All* of us?"

"Yes, *all* of us. We'll need to figure out sleeping arrangements, anyway."

Which could give him a chance to get the drop on her.

The look he shot her confirmed he knew what she was thinking.

She lifted her chin. "Where were you planning to sleep?"

"In one of the crew cabins."

"Fine. We will, too."

"Fine."

Isin pivoted on his heel and stalked up the dune.

She snatched up the empty drawstring bags and followed. Oh yeah, this was going to work out great.

Fifteen

"Nat, you awake?"

Nat rolled over to face Pete, who was seated on the bunk perpendicular to hers, keeping watch. Marlin was fast asleep across the room, in the bunk farthest from the crew cabin door. "Yeah, I'm awake." She'd slept fitfully for the past few hours, but mostly she'd been staring into space.

"How well do you know this Isin guy?"

She propped her head on her hand. Funny, she'd been wondering the same thing. "Not that well." And now she wasn't sure she knew him at all. "When we worked on the *Sphinx* together, he negotiated all our deals."

"Musta been good."

"He was. He made the ship profitable. But back then he wasn't..." She twirled her hand in the air, searching for the right word.

"Wasn't what?"

Only one word seemed to fit. "Menacing."

"How so?"

"That scar? He didn't have it. And his eyes weren't so... cold." She was still struggling to reconcile the predator prowling through the ship with the nonviolent negotiator she'd left in the torpedo bay.

"So what was he like back then?"

"Annoying. Argumentative. Anal." Actually, those traits hadn't really changed. "He thought he knew everything about everything, but when the Setarips attacked us, he fell apart.

Couldn't help me in the air, and was useless after we crashed, too."

"But you saved his life. Why?"

"I have no idea."

"You sure?"

She frowned. "What do you mean?"

"He was hurt after the crash, right?"

"Yeah."

"Would he have made it if you'd left him?"

"Probably not."

The corner of his mouth lifted. "You're a better person than you think."

She shook her head. "No, I'm not." He didn't understand. She'd done terrible things after the Setarips had captured her. Kidnapped people who'd died at Tnaryt's whim.

He shrugged. "So you say." He slid off the bunk and stood, grabbing his jacket and pulling it on. "Bottom line, he owes you. I'll make sure he remembers that."

She sat up. "Why are you defending me? We just met yesterday. I thought for sure you'd want me to take you back to Sage after Isin showed up."

He frowned. "Why?"

"Because dealing with mercenaries wasn't part of the job description."

"Not your fault they're here."

"But still—"

"They're bullies." He gave her a pointed look. "I can handle bullies." His half-smile returned. "Besides, you've kept your end of the deal. One day in and it's already an adventure."

She made a face.

His smile widened. "And this ship's a beauty. I'd do this job for free." He snagged one of the lanterns off the cabin's small desk and tucked his comm device into the pocket of his jacket. "I'll be in the engine room if you need me."

After he left, Nat pulled on her boots and paused for a quick glance in the mirror over the desk. Her turtleneck tunic and cargo pants were wrinkled and smudged, and her hair stuck out like porcupine quills. She couldn't do anything about her clothes without going out to *Gypsy*, but she smoothed her hair down with her fingers. Good enough.

Kneeling beside Marlin's bunk, she rested a hand on his shoulder. "Marlin?"

He woke with a start just like he had on *Gypsy*, arms flailing.

She backed out of striking distance. She needed to figure out a better way to rouse him. "It's okay. Just me."

He stopped thrashing and blinked at her in confusion.

"Pete's gone down to the engine room, and I'm heading to the bridge."

"Oh." He glanced around the room in surprise. "Guess I should get up." He said it like he hoped she'd talk him out of it.

"Your call. I just wanted you to know you'd be alone in here."

His expression shifted to alarm. "No, I'm awake." He scrambled out of bed and quickly yanked on his boots, bumping into the furniture in the process and letting loose with some colorful swearing.

She waited until he joined her, handing him a lantern that matched the one in her hand. They'd chosen one of the crew cabins on A deck not far from the exterior hatch. She'd closed and secured the hatch as best she could before sunrise, but having it open most of the night had freshened the air on this deck considerably.

However, fresh air wasn't a priority. Getting the bridge and engine room systems functional so they could take off—*that* was the priority.

With any luck, she could get in a few hours of solo time before Isin woke up. Walking the ship with him last night, giving him the rundown on the necessary repairs, had been damned uncomfortable. He'd double and triple checked her information, questioning everything. They'd debated the best way to proceed with the repairs. He'd argued for Kenji to work on the navigation console since he was a pilot, but she'd flatly refused. No one was touching that console except her. Certainly not a man she knew nothing about.

To break the stalemate, she'd finally agreed to have Isin work with her on the bridge repairs, instead. His presence wouldn't make her job any easier, but at least she wouldn't have to watch her back.

Stepping into the A deck corridor, she turned to Marlin. "Contact me with a progress report every two hours. If I don't hear from you, I'll come looking for you."

Some of the tension eased from his expression, just as she'd hoped it would. She hadn't made the request because she needed the information. She'd asked so he'd know she was watching out for him.

"Be careful," he warned.

"You, too."

He headed aft while she used her lantern to illuminate the dark corridor of A deck leading to the bridge. But when she reached the top of the stairway, her lantern's glow joined a flow of light spilling out of the bridge hatch onto the landing.

Isin crouched on the floor beside the tactical console. He glanced over his shoulder as she stepped through the hatch. "Orlov."

"Isin."

So he was back to calling her by her last name, huh? Good. It put them on equal footing again. She hadn't been comfortable with him calling her Natasha. The only person who'd ever used her full name was her mother.

She surveyed the bridge. He'd been busy while she'd slept. The deck was littered with damaged components and the remnants of the fried electrical system, like the aftermath of a mechanical war.

Isin gestured to the carnage. "This all needs to go to reclamation."

"Fine." She picked her way through the battlefield to the navigation console, tilting her lantern to get a better view. He'd pulled out the damaged nav unit, too. So much for her edict about being the only one who would touch it. Apparently he'd taken his role as her assistant as a green light to do whatever he wanted.

She pivoted to face him. "You removed the nav unit." And all the damaged wiring and connectors, too.

"And?"

"And, I told you I wanted to do that myself."

"You said you wanted to do the repairs. Now you can."

She ground her molars together. "I didn't want anyone else to touch it." He was acting way too heavy-handed with her ship.

He stared at her for a moment before standing and hauling a crate off the floor. Judging by the way his muscles flexed and bulged, it weighed as much as she did. He carried it over to her, using his boot to swipe debris out of his way, and set the box next to her with a thud.

"You'll need this."

She peered inside. The rebuilt nav unit she'd purchased for this console sat in the box, along with the other navigational items she'd picked up at Sage. He'd apparently consolidated everything she'd had stacked in the corridor on A deck and hauled it up to the bridge.

Damn him. Meeting his gaze, she spotted the flare of triumph in his dark eyes.

"Have at it. If you can manage."

The smirk that accompanied his comment made her blood boil, but the scar on his cheek turned the arrogant expression into something fearsome.

He didn't think she could handle it alone. And he could be right. Installing a major component was rarely a one-person job. But she'd strain every muscle in her arms and back before she'd give him the satisfaction of asking for his help.

Having tossed down his gauntlet, he grabbed an empty box, placed several large items of debris into it, snagged his lantern, and headed for the hatch.

As soon as he disappeared from sight, she stood. Hauling the component out of the crate took effort, but she managed. It hadn't seemed so heavy the day before when she'd had Marlin to help her carry it. Setting it on the deck, she inspected the unit and the console. Damn. He'd done a good job removing the damaged components. She'd hoped to find evidence of incompetence. Instead, it appeared he'd paid close attention last night when she'd described the problems with the system, and focused his considerable mental powers on dismantling everything correctly.

But that wasn't the biggest issue. To install the new unit, she'd have to hold it in place with one hand while attaching it with the other.

She glanced at the old unit sitting on the deck behind her. Isin would have had to do the same thing when he'd removed the damaged component. No wonder he'd looked so smug. He knew exactly how hard this would be for her.

Fine. She'd prove to him she could do it.

She had to sit on the deck to maneuver the bulky component into place, adjusting her grip and position to get as much leverage as possible. Shifting her shoulder under the unit to brace it, she slipped one hand free.

The unit started to slide.

She pushed up with both hands, pinning it in place. Changing the angle of her shoulder, she tried again. One hand free and... the unit moved.

"Dammit." She scooted forward and lay on her back, but her arms weren't long enough to hold the component in place. Kneeling and crouching didn't help, either. She simply didn't have the body mass or strength necessary to keep the unit stable while holding it with one hand.

Blowing out a breath, she lowered the component to the deck and rolled her neck and shoulders. She wasn't used to feeling weak. Not a pleasant sensation. Worse yet, her failure highlighted Isin's physical superiority. She could bluster and protest all she wanted, but in truth the only reason she wasn't trussed up in *Gypsy*'s cargo hold right now was because he was allowing her to stay out of a sense of obligation. She wasn't in control here. Not really.

Gritting her teeth, she reached for the unit. Maybe if she shoved one of the crates under it then—

She froze as the hairs on the back of her neck lifted.

She wasn't alone.

Her gaze darted to the hatch. The light from her lantern revealed Isin leaning against the landing's bulkhead, watching her. She hadn't even heard him climb the stairs.

"Need help?" His tone had changed, losing some of its edge. Not exactly friendly, but less confrontational.

She rested her elbows on her knees. Time to eat humble pie. "Yes."

He reached her in two strides.

She scooted back to give him room to maneuver.

Hefting the unit off the deck with ease, he settled onto his back, holding the component in place without so much as a groan.

She snagged her tools and crouched beside his prone form. She had to reach around him to attach the unit. No simple task. There was a lot of dark fabric and muscle in front of her nose. She did her best to ignore that fact as she focused on securing the unit in place, but she could feel him watching her.

She bobbled the last fastener, dropping it onto his chest. "Sorry." She snatched it up again.

"No problem." He didn't sound winded at all. He probably bench-pressed asteroids for fun.

She kept a firm grip on the fastener this time, locking it into place. She pushed away from the console. "That should do it."

He eased out from under the unit. "Can you handle it from here?" A small bead of sweat ran down the side of his face and disappeared beneath the collar of his tunic, the only indication that he'd exerted himself.

It drew her attention to several thin scars on his neck. Were those knife marks? Scratches?

He cleared his throat.

Busted! She'd been staring at him like he was an alien she'd just discovered. She glanced away. "Yeah. I've got it."

He pushed to his feet. "I'll finish the demo work. Let me know if you need any help." This time the words came out as a suggestion rather than a command.

She nodded. "I will."

He returned to the tactical console, adding more bits to the scraps on the deck.

She used the sleeve of her tunic to mop her brow. A turtleneck wasn't the ideal choice for working in such a small space. And the temperature seemed to be rising.

Nothing she could do about it now. Turning to the nav console, she pulled several items out of the crate Isin had given her and got to work.

The steady clink and clack of metal on metal counted out the time as they focused on their respective tasks. Her comband pinged with a message from Marlin, letting her know breakfast was ready in the galley. After relaying the information to Isin, she sent a short reply, telling Marlin she'd be down a little later. She was having too much fun working on the nav console to stop for food. She barely noticed when Isin left with another box of scrap.

She was sorting through the other boxes lining the bulkhead, looking for the mini-generator she'd purchased, when he returned carrying two steel containers and two drink canisters.

He held out one of the canisters. "Thought you might need some water."

He'd brought her water? That was a first. "Thanks." Raising the canister to her lips, she took a healthy swallow, the cool liquid sliding down her throat. "Did you get these from your ship?" The canisters certainly hadn't come from *Gypsy*.

He shook his head. "From the galley. Kenji hooked up our portable water purifier to the onboard water tanks."

"Oh." One problem solved.

He leaned against the bulkhead. "It'll be a while before we have enough filtered water for anything other than drinking and cooking, though. No showers."

She shrugged. Nothing new to her. While on Tnaryt's ship, showers hadn't been an option. An occasional sponge bath had been the best she'd managed, and those had been rare. This situation wasn't a hardship.

"I also brought food." He gestured to the two containers. "Brooks was afraid you might skip breakfast."

"I'll have something in a bit." Food was the farthest thing from her mind. "Did you check on Pete and Shash?"

"Briefly. They're making progress."

"Any issues?"

"Nope."

Huh. So the crews were actually working well together? Hard to believe after the way they'd met.

"Brooks and Kenji also reported the sanitation system for the A deck WC is functional. If you need to—"

"Good to know." She really didn't want to discuss her bathroom habits with him.

His gaze flicked to the navigation console. "How's it coming?"

"I was about to hook up the generator to test the circuits."

"Don't let me stop you." Pushing away from the wall, he set his water canister on top of the tactical console.

Nat located the generator and carried it to the nav console, pausing to push up her sleeves before settling onto the deck. The temperature on the bridge had definitely risen. After she finished testing the unit, she'd take a break and go below decks where it would be cooler.

A flash of movement in her peripheral vision made her turn.

Isin stood by the captain's chair with his back to her. He'd pulled his tunic over his head and tossed it on the seat.

She inhaled sharply. *Oh, Isin.*

He turned. "What?"

She couldn't answer him. Her throat had constricted when she'd caught sight of what his tunic had concealed.

She'd believed the scar on his face was bad. And it was. But the multitude of slashes covering his torso made him look like he'd been mauled by a lion. Repeatedly.

He glanced down before meeting her gaze. Ice frosted his words. "Don't like what you see?"

She swallowed, but it didn't help. She couldn't get her vocal chords to work. "What—" Her throat tightened. She tried again. "What happened?"

He braced his hands on his hips so his chest was on full display—as if he was daring her to look away. "Mercenary work is profitable. But not for the faint of heart."

She traced the pattern of wounds across his dark skin. Each one had been caused by—

"Believe me, most of my opponents looked far worse."

Bile rose in her throat. The people who'd inflicted those wounds had been fighting for their lives. And lost. To him.

Breathing became a real challenge. Her arms trembled. Her *whole body* trembled. She had to get out of here. Now.

Shoving to her feet, she snatched up the box he'd been loading with debris and hefted it in front of her like a shield. "I'll take this load." She edged toward the hatch.

She wasn't fooling him. The steel in his gaze told her he knew exactly why she was leaving.

"I'll be back," she mumbled as she stepped through the hatch.

His lips twisted in a cruel imitation of a smile. "I'll be here."

Sixteen

By some miracle she made it to the reclamation room without tripping over her own feet. She'd forgotten to bring a lantern, so she'd used her comband to light the way.

Her insides were still doing barrel rolls. How was she supposed to shrug this off? She'd been able to push Isin's job choice to the back of her mind while they'd focused on the ship repairs. But those scars—

She emptied her load into the open bin. It wouldn't process the raw materials until they got the electrical system working, but at least the pieces weren't cluttering up the bridge.

The bridge. She didn't want to go back there. Not while the evidence of his violent actions were on full display.

And what about your actions?

She flinched. Isin's voice, this time in her head. Ironically, while she'd lived with the Setarips, she'd come to rely on that voice as her conscience.

As usual, the voice was right. Who was she to judge him? Her hands were covered with blood, too. She may not have killed anyone directly, but she hadn't tried to stop Tnaryt. At least, not until Aurora had shown up.

She sagged against the bulkhead and closed her eyes, forcing her lungs to draw in slow, steady breaths. Debating with herself was a bad habit that never got her anywhere. She needed to get back to work.

However, she took the long route, using the aft stairs to reach A deck and making a stop at the crew WC before continuing toward the bridge. Maybe she should start working on the internal wiring from the bridge to the engine room. She could let him work on the tactical console and comm system while she repaired the connections in the corridors and access tunnels.

Coward.

Yep.

She slowed her steps, rehearsing what she was going to say as she made her way up the stairs to the bridge. She found Isin on his back, wedged under the tactical console. Good. She wouldn't have to look at him. "I'm going to start repairing the electrical lines from the bridge to the engine room."

"Fine."

She blinked. Was he really not going to give her an argument? He'd challenged her about everything else. Why not this? Her gaze swept the bridge, looking for anything that might explain why he wasn't putting up a fight. But she came up empty. "Well, I'll go then."

He grunted in response.

She gathered the tools and supplies she'd need, as well as the water and food he'd brought her and the lantern she'd forgotten last time.

When she reached A deck, she took a few minutes to eat, more to keep up her strength than because she was hungry. That chore accomplished, she focused on the access panel for the A deck landing.

The interior was marred by scorch marks from the electrical fire that had followed the surge of electricity along the conduits. The ship's fire-suppression system had contained the fire inside the bulkheads, but she had a lot of wiring to replace.

Pulling out her tools, she set to work, following the path of destruction along A deck, crawling into access tunnels and removing panels. The task succeeded in distracting her—mostly. But she kept listening for the sound of Isin's footsteps.

By the time she was ready to quit for the day, her muscles were pleasantly sore and her mind considerably calmer. And she'd completed all the work on A deck and moved to B deck. She also hadn't seen any sign of Isin, Kenji, or Shash. Marlin had brought her some food in the late afternoon, which she suspected he'd used as an excuse to visually verify she was still alive and well.

He'd also grumbled that Kenji had kept stopping by the galley, and had appointed himself as Marlin's official taste tester. Apparently Kenji's attitude hadn't been appreciated.

A light bobbed up the stairs toward her as she headed for D deck to check on Pete. She recognized Marlin's shuffling walk even before she saw his face in the lantern's glow. "Everything okay?"

He stifled a yawn. "Just tired." He looked like he was barely keeping his eyes open. "Plumbing repairs are done. Just waiting on power."

"That's great. You heading to the cabin?"

"Uh-huh."

"I'll be up as soon as I check on Pete." She should probably track down Isin, too, but she didn't want to ruin her mellow mood.

Tapping noises drew her toward the engine room, where two pairs of boots stuck out from under one of the turbines.

"How's it coming?"

Pete's voice overlaid what sounded like a sarcastic comment from Shash. "Goin' good. Should have this part done in another hour."

"It's getting late. You might want to call it for today."

"How late?"

"Almost ten."

"Really?" Pete worked his way out from under the turbine. "Hadn't realized." His eyes sparkled and his face was smeared with gunk, making him look like a kid who'd been playing in the mud.

"Having fun?"

"Oh, yeah. This ship's got a great design. Workin' on her is a treat."

That comment earned a muffled snort from Shash. "It's a pain in the ass."

Pete grinned at Nat, making him look even more like a kid. Lowering his voice, he leaned closer. "She won't admit it, but she's in love, too."

Nat had trouble imagining Shash in love with anything—except her own negativity. "Don't let me stop you if—"

"Nah." He stretched, his back letting out an audible pop. "I could use some shut-eye. I'll be up in a few minutes."

"Okay."

Light flowed out of the cabin on A deck when Nat returned. Marlin sat on his bunk, staring at the doorway. His body jerked when he saw her. "I didn't hear you coming."

No wonder. Ever since they'd encountered Isin's crew, she'd fallen back into the habit of moving with stealth. "Didn't mean to startle you."

"I know." But he still looked jumpy.

"Anything wrong?"

"Not exactly. I ran into Kenji out in the corridor. He was coming down the ladder."

"Oh?"

"Yeah. Apparently he was working on repairing the outer hatch. He also rigged a camouflage piece so when the hatch is closed from the inside, the outside still looks covered in sand."

"He told you that?"

"No. I climbed up and took a look after he went into his cabin."

Her lips quirked up. "Sneaky."

"Just keeping an eye on things." And speaking of eyes, his lids were drooping. "Guess I'll turn in."

He stretched out on his side, facing her, and closed his eyes. But after a moment, he opened them again. "Did you come up with a plan to thwart them yet?"

Nat sat on her bunk to pull off her boots. "No. But I will." Now that she was seeing the ship coming together, there was no way she'd let it slip through her fingers.

Marlin sighed, closing his eyes again. "I think they're gonna take it from us," he mumbled.

She paused with one boot in her hand, her pulse kicking up a notch. "Why do you say that?"

But his breathing had already evened out, his face relaxing in sleep.

She set the boot on the floor without making a sound. "Over my dead body."

Seventeen

A dark shape loomed out of the darkness, reaching for her. Nat lashed out, deflecting the attack and stumbling as the ground shifted under her feet. Loose sand pulled at her boots while light from her comband swept across the moving shadow, revealing orange and black scales surrounding eyes like a cat's. The Setarip's clawed hand encircled her throat, choking her as he lifted her off her feet.

She scratched and kicked, struggling to free herself. "Miiiiinnnne."

The sinister hiss sent tremors through her body, even as her mind rebelled. This wasn't real. Tnaryt was dead.

She kicked again, aiming for his chest. This time her blow connected, but it was like kicking stone. He yanked her closer, his face changing before her eyes, the scales giving way to dark skin marred by a jagged scar. The dead calm in Isin's eyes chilled her to the bone.

"Maybe I wasn't clear. It's mine."

Light glinted off a razor-sharp blade. He plunged it toward her heart.

No!

Nat snapped awake, gasping for air as she pressed her palm to her chest. Her heart raced and her entire body shook in the aftermath of the dream.

"Nat? What's wrong?" Pete appeared by her bedside, the soft glow from the lantern on the desk casting his features in shadow.

She took a few calming breaths. "Nightmare."

"Thought so." He was silent for a moment. "Wanna talk about it?"

"No." And she wouldn't be going back to sleep either. Not with that image burned into her brain.

She reached for her comband and checked the time. Half past two. She'd only been in bed four hours. Great. She shoved the blanket aside and stood. "I'm going to the bridge."

Pete watched her, his face lined with concern. "You want company?"

"That's okay. We shouldn't leave Marlin alone." The man in question was still dead to the world, a soft snore rumbling from his bunk. If he woke up and discovered they were gone, he'd panic.

Pete nodded, settling back onto his bunk.

She grabbed one of the lanterns and exited into the passageway.

She glanced at the ladder to the outer hatch. The lure of fresh air and a view of the stars called to her, but Isin, Kenji, and Shash had chosen to share a cabin nearby. If they heard the hatch opening in the middle of the night, goodness only knew what kind of reaction that might trigger.

Instead, she climbed the stairs to the bridge. Adjusting the lantern to its lowest setting, she placed it on the navigation console in front of her and dropped into the chair.

Her muscles slowly unwound the knots lining her shoulders and back. Sitting at the controls always calmed her. She belonged here. A flight with *Gypsy* would do wonders for her mental state, but that was even less of an option than stargazing.

Leaning back, she pivoted to the right and surveyed the compact bridge. Isin had been busy. All the debris had been cleared away and the tactical console looked almost normal. She glanced at the captain's chair by the aft bulkhead. Funny, but she hadn't even considered sitting in it. Didn't even want to. In her daydreams about this ship, she'd always pictured herself at the helm. She hadn't envisioned a separate captain's chair, but of course the ship had one. Maybe she'd remove it.

Pivoting back around, she stroked her fingers over the controls. She wanted this ship with every fiber of her being. But first she had to deal with the man standing in her way.

What exactly had happened to him after she'd been captured? In her experience, people didn't change—not really. And yet Isin had made a one hundred eighty degree shift in the year they'd been apart. Who was he now? The prickly perfectionist she'd saved, or the fearsome fighter he'd become?

She stared at the ceiling, but the answers weren't written on the smooth surface. Was her nightmare a warning? Was her subconscious telling her that Isin posed as much of a threat as Tnaryt had? Or was she overreacting?

And how far was she prepared to go to keep this ship? Steal it? Wage war on Isin and his crew? If push came to shove, could she be as ruthless as he seemed to be?

She drew her knees up, wrapping her arms around her legs. She'd hoped the darkness had ended when Tnaryt's ship had been destroyed. Instead, it had followed her here. And if she—

The soft thump of footsteps on the stairs jarred her out of her mental orbit. She turned to face the hatch just as Isin's dark form appeared in the opening.

He halted, the glow from his lantern casting his face in a pattern of light and shadow that made his expression difficult to read. "I didn't expect you to be here."

"I couldn't sleep."

"Neither could I."

He didn't move. They stared at each other, the silence stretching out, broken only by the soft whisper of their breathing.

He took a step back. "I'll go—"

"It's okay." She licked her dry lips. "You can stay."

He tilted his head. "You sure?"

No. "Yeah."

He waited for a moment, as if giving her a chance to change her mind. When she didn't, he turned off his lantern and settled into the tactical chair.

The pose was so familiar, reminding her more of the man she'd saved than the monster from her nightmare. Which brought to mind a question she'd wanted to ask since he'd arrived. "What happened to the bodies?"

"What bodies?"

"The original crew. The ones we saw when we were hiding from the Setarips."

"Ah." He let his head fall against the headrest with a sigh. "I buried them in the mountains."

"Why?" She hadn't expected that from him. He was in the business of killing people, not burying them. "You didn't know them."

His brows drew down. "I couldn't leave them on the ship."

"Well, no. But—"

"But I could have just dumped them outside and let the sand cover them. Is that what you're saying?" His voice took on an edge.

"Some people would." A mercenary certainly would. "Why didn't you?" She was genuinely curious.

"It didn't feel right. Not after—" He cut off abruptly.

She waited, but he didn't continue. "After what?"

He glanced away. "Nothing."

Uh-uh. He wasn't getting off that easy. "Come on, Isin. Tell me. After what?"

"After—" He stopped and cleared his throat. "After you sacrificed yourself. For me." The words came out slightly guttural.

She stared at him. Was he getting choked up? Over *her?* That didn't seem likely. But then again, nothing about this situation seemed likely.

His gaze swung back to her. "I never got a chance to thank you."

She almost fell out of her chair. Instead, she gripped the armrests. Maybe she'd fallen asleep and this was a different dream. She'd never imagined he'd say thank you. How was she supposed to respond to *that?*

He pivoted toward her, resting his elbows on his knees. "I should have died that day." The intensity of his gaze drilled into her. "I still can't believe you're here."

She responded without thinking. "Good thing I am. Someone has to keep your overblown ego in check."

He pulled back, staring at her.

She tensed. She'd gone too far. The old Isin would have answered with a snappy comeback. But this one might—

His lips lifted, the scar turning the gesture into a snarl. "You're good at that."

"What?"

"Keeping my ego in check."

She frowned. His voice didn't match his expression. He didn't sound menacing. He sounded... amused? It took her a moment to realize she could see his teeth. He was *smiling.* "Thank you."

His smile widened, the gesture no longer looking like a snarl. A soft chuckle rumbled out of his chest. "I sure have missed you, Natasha."

Heat climbed up her neck. Thank goodness he wouldn't be able to see her blush in the dim light. The darkness seemed to be loosening her tongue, too. "Of course you have. I'm a delightful person."

He snorted with laughter. *Laughter!* "And modest."

"It's my best quality."

The smile slowly faded, replaced with a look that made her stomach turn somersaults.

"I wouldn't say that."

Did the room just shrink? Isin hadn't moved, but he suddenly seemed to be filling her vision. And she couldn't look away.

Scrambling for something to break the tension, she tossed out the first thing that popped into her mind. "How's your sister?"

That did it. He sat back, his expression puzzled. "My sister?"

"Yes. The one who calls you El."

"You remembered that?"

"Of course I remembered. You were the last person I talked to before—" She didn't finish the sentence.

"Before the Setarips took you?"

She gave a curt nod. "Our conversation stuck in my mind."

The *look* crept back. "Mine, too."

Danger! She drew her knees to her chest, her legs creating a physical barrier between them. "How is she?"

"My sister? She's good."

"Is she on your ship?"

"Hell, no!"

His vehemence surprised her. "Then where is she?"

"In school. Getting her degree."

"In what?"

"Astrobiology."

Nat's brows lifted. She'd always suspected Isin came from an educated family, but this put a finer point on it. "So she's a scientist?"

"Yes. A very talented one."

"I'm not surprised." Her brother was no slouch in the brains department, either. "What does she think of your change in... profession?"

His expression closed down. "She doesn't know."

Nat stared at him. "You're kidding. She *has* to know. You two talk, don't you? She's seen you, right?"

"Yes."

"Then she knows."

His jaw worked, like he was grinding his teeth. "I didn't tell her."

She shook her head. How could he be so smart and so dense? "You don't have to. The scars, the muscles, the shaved head—they're not exactly subtle. Didn't she say anything to you about the changes?"

He pressed his lips together. "She was concerned about the scar on my face."

"How did you explain it?"

"I didn't."

"And she accepted that?"

"She's twenty-two. Just a kid. I don't want her thinking about death."

Just a kid? His sister was only two years younger than she was. "Maybe you should have considered that before changing professions."

He bristled. "She's getting the education she deserves. That's what matters."

The light bulb went off. "Is that why you became a mercenary? So you could pay for your sister's tuition?"

"It was a... factor." He shifted, the lantern's glow reflecting off his profile. He looked uncomfortable.

"Then why didn't you go the mercenary route from the beginning? If you needed money so badly, why take a job working for Mirko on the *Sphinx*? The ship wasn't even profitable until you came along. It wasn't exactly a good bet."

He didn't look at her. "Money was a factor. But not the only one."

His strange behavior drew her forward. She put her feet on the floor and rested her forearms on her thighs. "What then? What happened after I was captured that turned you into—" She swept her hand to encompass his whole body. "This."

The muscles of his neck and jaw flexed. When he finally met her gaze, the look in his eyes took her by surprise. As did his words.

"Why did you risk your life to save me?"

Now it was her turn to flinch.

"You could have left me. Hidden yourself where they wouldn't have found you. Instead, you made noise to draw them away from me. Why?"

How many times had she asked herself that exact same question? A thousand? Ten thousand? She'd lost count of the hours she'd spent contemplating her decision. And yet, she still didn't have an answer. "I don't know."

He mirrored her pose, less than a meter of space separating them. He held her gaze. "Don't you?"

Irritation flared. "No, I don't. Why? Do you?"

His eyes looked like molten glass in the lantern's glow. "You didn't want me to die."

"Of course I didn't. I don't want *anyone* to die."

"Do you make a habit out of risking your life to save others?"

She glared at him, but it was an empty gesture. He had her pinned. Self-preservation and guilt had motivated her to take risks since that day, but she couldn't use either excuse to explain away her actions regarding him. In fact, self-preservation should have driven her to abandon him.

"I'll take that as a no." For some reason, that seemed to please him.

She sat back, folding her arms over her chest. "I was under stress. And you were injured."

"I was a burden." He stated it as a fact. "You should have left me."

Was he seriously trying to convince her she'd made the wrong decision? "The Setarips would have killed you."

"I would have deserved it."

"Deserved it?"

"It was my fault. I was so preoccupied with self-pity while I was on the *Sphinx* that I didn't bother to spend a few hours learning how to operate *Gypsy*'s systems. If I had, I could have helped you escape the Setarips. Instead, I panicked, we crashed, I got injured, and you got captured." An emotion that looked suspiciously like remorse flashed across his face. "The Setarips could have killed *you*."

Huh. In a roundabout way, he was apologizing. She hadn't expected that.

"Why didn't they?"

"Kill me?" She could answer that one. "They needed a pilot for cargo runs."

His brows lifted. "That's what you were doing while you were with them? Making cargo runs?"

"That, and fixing the engines."

"Fixing the engines? Why?"

She was unwilling to dredge up the memories. "It's a long story."

He studied her. "How did you escape?"

"I had help."

"From Brooks and Stevens?"

She shook her head. "Marlin was a captive, like me. And Pete and I just met at Sage a few days ago."

"Really?" Isin's eyes narrowed. "He seems very—protective—for such a short acquaintance."

"He's a good guy."

"How good?"

She frowned. "Best mechanic in Sage from what I've seen."

Some of the tension eased from his expression. "Shash would agree."

Nat snorted. "Nice to know she agrees with me on *something.*"

"She's a little rough. I'll give you that."

Said the guy who looked like he ate razor blades for breakfast.

"She also knows her stuff. Her father was an engineer."

That surprised her. "Do you trust her?"

"Not for a minute. But she'll follow orders as long as there's no profit in disobeying them."

"And if there is?"

He held her gaze. "I won't let her harm you."

Not where she was going with her question, but good to know. Part of the reason she, Marlin, and Pete had decided to share a cabin was because Nat had visions of waking up to the slice of Shash's blade across her throat. "What about this ship? Will she try to take it when it's operational?"

The corners of his lips turned down. "She can't fly it."

She didn't like the way he said it. "Can *you?*" He certainly hadn't known anything about flying when they'd made their last cargo delivery together.

"No. But Kenji can."

He wasn't making her feel any better. "Are you going to take the ship from me?"

"No."

"That's good—"

"But I promised it to my crew."

Heat flared in her belly. "So did I."

"I doubt Brooks or Stevens would gut you if you failed to deliver it."

Her mouth dropped open. "Are you saying your crew *would?*"

"They might."

She sputtered to get her words out. "What kind of people are you working with, Isin?"

He lifted one brow. "Mercenaries."

And he was one of them. He'd told her he'd keep her safe from Shash, but that depended on maintaining control of the ship. Where did that leave her?

She stood, lifting the lantern off the console. "I'm going to bed."

He rose, too, towering over her without even trying. "Natasha—"

She sidestepped to the hatch. "It's late. Or early. I'm tired."

He didn't try to stop her as she left. "We'll find a solution," he called after her.

"Sure we will," she called back. She didn't believe it for a second.

Eighteen

Nat didn't sleep well, but four hours later she was back on the bridge, working on the navigation console.

Isin worked beside her, but they hadn't spoken more than a few words to each other. Whatever rapport they'd had during the night had evaporated. A low-grade tension filled the room, the awkwardness pushing them apart, especially whenever they got in each other's way.

At midday she fled to the galley, staying longer than necessary to finish her meal. Marlin indulged her in conversation while he sorted items in the pantry.

On her way back to the bridge, she passed Isin on the stairway.

"Itorye just reported in."

The name meant nothing to her. "Who's Itorye?"

"My first mate. *Vengeance* is in orbit."

Her breath stuttered. "Oh." Now he had reinforcements. A whole ship full of mercenaries, fresh from the kill.

"As soon as the sun sets, I'll be leaving."

"Leaving?" She hadn't expected that.

"Byrd's coming down in one of our troop transports to pick me up. Itorye and I have a few matters to discuss and Shash has given me a list of parts to buy in Sage."

Which would give him more leverage. Up until now she'd been the one financing the repairs. "Shash and Kenji aren't going with you?"

"No, they'll be staying here."

A tremor danced under her skin. "Is that wise?"

"It'll be fine. Shash has no interest in being stranded here. She won't give you any problems."

She didn't share his confidence. Tonight they'd reinstate their sleep rotations. Or maybe she'd forego sleep altogether. "Will you be bringing more of your crew down?"

His eyes narrowed at her tone. "Maybe. Is that a problem?"

"Why would it be a problem?" *Other than the fact you want my ship?*

"You tell me."

"I just want to know what to expect, that's all."

"Expect *me* at sunset tomorrow."

"Fine."

"Fine."

She brushed past him, climbing the stairs to the bridge.

Of course *he* wouldn't see anything wrong with bringing more crew onboard. Correction. Bringing more bloodthirsty mercenaries. He *owed* them a ship. *Her* ship. If he thought they coveted it now, just wait until they got a closer look.

But he owed *her* more, dammit. Without her, he'd be dead. She deserved this ship. He'd brought this problem down on her. He needed to fix it.

She spent the afternoon working on the B deck electrical connections, but her heart wasn't in it. She managed to bang her arm and her forehead in the space of five minutes because she couldn't concentrate. She kept getting distracted by thoughts of mutiny by Shash, Kenji, or whomever else Isin might bring down from *Vengeance.*

Isin tracked her down in the infirmary, where she was taping up a cut on her hand that wouldn't stop bleeding.

"I'm taking off."

She wiggled her free fingers in his direction, but didn't look up from her task. "Safe travels."

"Do you need help?"

"Nope." She kept working.

"Anything else before I go?"

She shook her head.

"I'll be back the same time tomorrow."

"Fine."

He might have sighed. Or it might have been the scrape of his boot on the deck as he left.

She paused, listening until his steps faded before lowering her arms and closing her eyes. Blissful silence. But tension followed right on its heels. With Isin off the ship, she'd have to keep a close watch on Shash and Kenji. She wasn't too concerned about Kenji. Despite Marlin's grumbling, nothing had happened between them that sounded an alarm.

Shash was another matter. No telling what she might get up to without Isin present to supervise. Like staging a little accident.

Cheery thought.

What if Shash *did* try to take her out? Maybe her best defense was a good offense.

Pushing to her feet, she snagged her lantern and made her way to the engine room. She picked up snippets of conversation between Pete and Shash as she approached.

"...best machine until the four hundred killed it," Pete said.

"You're spaced," Shash replied. "The four hundred was way better than the three."

"How do you figure? The pressure regulator wasn't–
"

"Hey, Pete," Nat called out as she stepped into the room.

Pete's head and torso appeared from around one of the bulkheads. "Hey, Nat. Somethin' wrong?"

"No. I just wanted to see how things are going."

"Goin' fine. We'll be runnin' prelim tests on the electrical tonight. After you finish repairin' the wirin', we should be able to get power to the bridge."

"Really?" They were making faster progress than she'd anticipated. "I'll make that my priority." She paused. "Isin's gone. Won't be back until tomorrow night."

Pete nodded. "Already stopped by and told us." He gave her a look filled with significance. "We'll keep things runnin' smooth here."

She forced a small smile. He might believe Shash wasn't a threat, but she didn't agree. "I'll leave you to it."

She stopped by the galley and grabbed snacks she could nibble while she worked, informing Marlin she didn't plan to sleep much tonight. Instead, she'd power through the electrical repairs. Shash couldn't lay a trap if she didn't know where to find her.

She lost track of time as she crawled through the access tunnels. Most of the repairs were straightforward, but one section on C deck proved challenging. The fire had ripped through here, destroying not just the electrical, but many of the components around it. She'd purchased new parts, but the tight quarters made removal and replacement difficult.

To install the new transformer, she had to stretch out on the tunnel's decking, not the most comfortable position. And whoever had designed the ship hadn't anticipated the need for making repairs without the benefit of the automatic lighting system. She had to use her lantern

and comband in combination, which generated harsh
shadows. Within minutes her neck and shoulder muscles
knotted up.

She rolled onto her back to give her arms a rest
and focused on relaxing her muscles. The whisper of voices
reached her, drifting in through the ventilation grate.

"...is a good idea. And maybe the cook. But she's got
to go." Shash's voice.

Nat tensed.

"Cap won't ditch her," Kenji replied. "They have
history. She's the reason we're on this boat."

"So we're stuck with her?"

"We'll need another pilot and Cap says she's a good
one. Why pay when we can have her for free?"

Nat's jaw dropped open.

Shash sounded somewhat mollified. "And if they put
up a fuss, we'll press them into service?"

"That's the plan."

A dull roar filled Nat's ears. Isin was planning to
kidnap her? *Force* her and her crew to work for him?

"I knew he had to be playing her."

Nat bit down on her tongue to stop her indignant
screech.

Kenji grunted. "Keep a lid on it, okay? We've got a
lot of work to do before then."

Nat's stomach lurched. Being stranded on Troi would
have been bad enough. But this—

Shash's voice started to fade as she and Kenji
continued down the corridor. "You worry about yourself. I'm
great at keeping secrets."

She didn't catch Kenji's reply. Not that she cared.
She couldn't move a muscle, but her thoughts raced at light
speed.

She was an idiot. She'd actually *believed* Isin. Believed *in* Isin. But it was all a smokescreen. She'd been manipulated by the best negotiator in the quadrant.

And he'd keep her in the dark as long as he could. Who knew what elaborate fabrication he'd conjure? He might even try to convince her he was offering her a job. She'd bought everything he'd told her so far. Why wouldn't he expect more of the same?

She needed to talk to Pete and Marlin. But first she had to finish this repair so they could get power to the bridge. She'd need that advantage for what she had in mind. Isin thought he'd cornered her, but she was about to show him she was a moving target. And that she had more than a few tricks up her sleeve.

Nineteen

"They're going to do *what!?*"

Nat made a shushing sound to Marlin and glanced at the closed cabin door. Odds were good Shash and Kenji wouldn't hear them even if they were standing outside with their ears pressed to the door, but she wasn't taking any chances. Too much was at stake.

"As soon as the repairs are complete, they're going to force us into becoming part of their crew."

Pete's normally sunny expression had darkened like a thundercloud. "Force us how, exactly?"

"I don't know. Negotiation, manipulation, coercion, threat of violence. Whatever will work, I suspect."

Marlin's eyes rounded, his face draining of color. "We'll leave. Tonight." He started to rise but Nat put a restraining hand on his arm.

"*We're* not going anywhere. This is *our* ship. That hasn't changed."

He stared at her. "*Everything's* changed. This ship isn't worth becoming a prisoner again."

"I won't let that happen."

"How? They have a ship in orbit. We're completely outnumbered."

"Only in a fair fight. I don't intend to fight fair." Because Isin certainly wasn't. "But I'll need your help."

"What kind of help?"

"You know a lot about herbs. Is there any chance you could come up with a way to drug Isin's crew?"

His voice squeaked. "Drug them?"

"Yes. Unless you have a better idea for putting them out of commission."

"I... I don't know. I've never tried to drug anyone before."

"Would any of the herbs you bought work?"

He shook his head. "They're flavorings. Worst they could do is give someone indigestion."

Damn. If they couldn't incapacitate the crew—

"But there might be tranquilizers or sedatives in the ship's infirmary that I could slip into their food or water."

Now they were talking. "Even better. See what you can find. Pete, I need your help installing kill switches on the bridge and in the engine room that we can control remotely."

Pete ran his hand along the scruff on his chin. "Installin' 'em wouldn't be hard. But controllin' by remote? We ain't got nothin' onboard to do that."

Nat lifted her forearm. "I was hoping we could tie them into my comband."

The corners of his mouth lifted. "Oh. Well, yeah, that might do."

Nat unfastened the band and handed it to him. "Make whatever modifications you need to, but we have to get the devices installed tonight. I won't have any trouble on the bridge with Isin gone, but I don't know about engineering. Will Shash be down there?"

Pete shook his head. "She was lookin' forward to a full night's sleep."

"Perfect. If you can get me what we need, I'll head up to the bridge."

Within fifteen minutes she had the small pack of materials in her hands. Marlin had gone down to the infirmary on B deck, while Pete was working in the engine room.

Installing the kill switch in the nav console and building the connections around it so that it was concealed took most of her attention, but the pain of Isin's betrayal overlaid every move she made, poking her like an emotional splinter. After she'd tested the switch with the generator, she checked on Marlin, who was standing in the infirmary, inspecting a row of bottles on the counter. He glanced over his shoulder as the light from her lantern reached him.

"What did you find?" she asked.

"Just what we need, I think." He handed her one of the bottles. "It's a sleep aid."

She read the content information printed on the side of the bottle. "Looks promising."

"Yeah. The only question will be whether it's still effective after all this time. And whether I can mask the taste. It's in pill form now."

"The seal's still intact, so it should be fine. What about the others?" She gestured to the three bottles sitting on the counter.

He shrugged. "Decoys. In case Shash or Kenji showed up and asked what I was doing. I was going to pretend I was looking for something to help with a headache."

His ingenuity made her smile. "Marlin, you're a gem. Thank you."

He headed for the galley with the bottle in hand while she joined Pete in the engine room. He'd completed his kill switch installation and was working on the modifications to her comband.

He held up the device. "Never seen one this fancy before."

"It was a gift."

He accepted her answer without question. "Well, it'll work nice. Just about done." He keyed in a few more commands and the device pinged. Powering up the generator connected to the engine console, he tapped the comband. The console immediately went dark.

"You did it!" Nat lowered her voice to a stage whisper. "What kind of effective range will it have?"

"Once the ship's electrical and comm systems are runnin'? A kilometer at least, maybe more."

Better than she'd hoped for. "Thanks, Pete."

He shook his head, his gaze somber. "No need for thanks. Isin ain't got no right to take this ship from you. Or force you to work for him. I aim to stop him any way I can."

His unwavering loyalty rendered her speechless, so she gave him a quick hug instead.

But rather than following him back to the cabin, she decided to finish the electrical repairs that Shash and Kenji's conversation had interrupted. Pete didn't question her decision—he seemed to understand she needed the distraction more than sleep.

Besides, working was the only way to drive thoughts of Isin out of her head. She'd trusted him, believed in him. Worked side by side on this ship that had saved him. And all along he'd been plotting against her.

It was a lousy way to pay her back for her sacrifice. Taking the ship out from under him wouldn't balance the scales—not by a long shot—but at least it would get her what she wanted. And show him just how much he'd underestimated her.

Twenty

"Natasha."

A deep voice was calling her name.

"Wake up, Natasha."

Nat pried her eyes open, focusing on the figure standing over her. *Isin.*

She frowned. Why was she lying on the deck of the bridge? And why was he here?

He stepped back, the glow from the bridge's overhead lights illuminating his features in vivid detail. Pete and Shash had completed the electrical tests that morning, restoring the ship's interior lighting. She'd come to the bridge after—

The memory of the previous night's activities registered, pushing a burning anger through her body. She fought to keep her expression neutral. "I fell asleep."

"I can see that."

She put down the tools she'd been clutching and slid out from under the nav console, staying as far away from him as the confined quarters of the bridge would allow.

"Any issues?" He looked her up and down, his gaze assessing.

His scrutiny only added fuel to the fire. "With what?"

His brows lifted at her tone. "With Shash and Kenji."

No, my issue is with YOU! "No problems."

"So you're not napping up here because of them?"

"I wasn't napping. I fell asleep."

He frowned. "Are you always this grumpy when you wake up?"

"Only when someone badgers me," she snapped. She wasn't helping her cause, but she couldn't seem to control her tongue.

He was silent for a long moment. "I didn't come up here to argue with you."

"Then why did you?"

"I have a proposition for you."

Warning lights flashed behind her eyes. "What kind of proposition?"

"I talked to Itorye about our situation and she came up with a solution."

I'll bet she did. "Which is?"

"I hire you as the pilot and captain for this ship, flying under my command."

Her stomach rolled. Just what she'd expected.

"As captain, you'd have a fair amount of autonomy, and you'd make a lot more money than you would running freight."

The knots in her stomach tightened. "So, you'd pay me?"

"Of course I'd pay you."

Of course. Or at least that's what he'd promise her until he had her under his thumb.

"What about Marlin and Pete?"

"I'd hire them, too. You'd be in charge of the crew on this ship. But you wouldn't be expected to—*participate*—in our work except to get the ship and crew where we need them to be."

"And *Gypsy?*"

"She'd stay on this ship. With you."

"Would she be used for your... work?"

His gaze flickered. "That would be up to you."

She barely contained a derisive snort. As soon as they were in the air, *Gypsy* would become yet another resource he had commandeered.

"Well?" He held her gaze, waiting for her response.

What a pretty picture he was painting—for him. But his plan had two major flaws. He was still taking command of her ship. And it was all a manipulative lie.

She'd have to tread carefully. Her hostility had already given away more than she'd planned. "I'll think about it."

Clearly not the answer he'd wanted. "It would allow you to keep the ship."

Hardly. She'd be working as his servant. Or slave.

"You don't look happy."

Happy? She wasn't even on speaking terms with happy. "It's a lot to think about."

He nodded slowly, although he didn't seem to be buying her excuse. "And you haven't had much sleep. I shouldn't have sprung it on you."

Oh, but he was planning to spring a lot more on her later. She turned away. "I'm going down to the galley."

He stepped back to let her pass. "Why don't you call it a night."

She stopped in her tracks. Was that how this would go down? He'd get her safely tucked in her cabin and then spring his trap? Maybe he wasn't going to wait until the ship was operational. "Did you bring anyone from your ship with you?"

He frowned at her non sequitur. "No. In fact, Byrd took the *Dagger* back to *Vengeance*."

"The *Dagger*?"

"The ship we flew here."

"What about the troop transport?" He'd said his pilot was coming down in a troop transport. Had he brought a battalion of mercenaries with him?

"He took them both. The *Dagger* pairs well with most ships so they can be flown as one vessel."

Right. Because a mercenary would need that kind of functionality. Either that, or he was lying through his teeth.

"*Vengeance* needs some repairs, so Itorye's keeping the ship in orbit while the crew completes them."

Finally some good news. "How long will their repairs take?"

"A few days."

"Oh." Not much time, but she'd take every hour she could get. She turned back to the hatch.

"Natasha?"

Stop calling me that! She bit down on her tongue. "What?"

"I'll need your answer before then."

She kept her expression benign. "You'll have it." And a whole lot more.

She escaped down the stairs as quickly as she could. The overhead illumination brightened the stairwell, reflecting off the white bulkheads and creating a cheerful ambiance that was at complete odds with her dark mood.

When she reached the C deck corridor, her grip on her emotions slipped and she sagged against the bulkhead. How could Isin treat her like this, after all she'd done to save him?

But she knew the answer. It was as plain as the scar on his face. Isin—the man she'd known—didn't exist anymore. He'd died on this ship. The person standing on her bridge was a wraith, stripped of all compassion and empathy. She'd do well to remember that.

Shoving away from the wall, she made her way to the galley. She'd hoped to find Marlin or Pete there, but the room was empty. Opening a storage cabinet, she grabbed one of the meal packs Marlin had laid in for the crew. She consumed the food on autopilot, chewing and swallowing only because her body needed fuel to function.

Isin had said it would take a few days before his ship would be repaired. If she, Pete, and Marlin pushed themselves, maybe they could get this ship ready to fly before then. They'd also have to drug Isin, Kenji, and Shash to take them out of the equation, but she was counting on Marlin's ingenuity. And unassuming manner. They'd never suspect him of duplicity.

Her immediate food needs taken care of, she headed for D deck. Exhaustion pulled at her, but she refused to follow Isin's order to get some sleep. There was another important task she had to accomplish before this ship left its sand cocoon. *Gypsy* needed a home in the ship's bay. It was high time Nat gave her one.

Twenty-One

Nat didn't want to close her eyes.

Variations on the nightmare she'd had featuring Tnaryt and Isin had played in a loop in her dreams the past two nights. Each time, she'd woken in a sweat, every muscle tensed. When she went back to sleep, the dream would repeat itself, details changing but the outcome always the same. Anxiety stalked her throughout the day, especially when she was working on the bridge with Isin. Keeping her emotions in check was getting harder with each passing hour.

She was also struggling to keep a civil tongue whenever they spoke. Everything he said fueled her anger, so she ignored him as much as possible. Which was kind of like ignoring a rhinoceros in a tree house.

So far, she'd managed to keep from giving him an answer regarding his proposal. She'd have to say yes eventually, just to keep him from taking action against her, but she'd also have to be convincing. If he spotted a lie, everything would unravel. The nightmares and lack of sleep weren't helping.

Despite her personal demons, the repairs were going well. The new supplies Isin had brought had allowed for a leap forward. Kenji had finished the repair on the outer hatch, which now locked and sealed, Pete and Shash were making steady progress in the engine room, and she'd finished the work on the navigation console, moving on to the damaged comm system. If she finished that today, she could leave the rest of the bridge work to Isin and go help Pete in the engine room.

Her willingness to work in the same space as Shash, rather than Isin, said a lot about her state of mind.

She took time to plaster the most neutral expression she could manage onto her face before climbing the stairs to the bridge. Greeting Isin with a scowl only increased his scrutiny.

It was wasted effort. When she stepped onto the bridge, *he* was the one scowling. At *her*.

"Want to explain this?" He held up a small object.

"Explain wh—" The word lodged in her throat as she recognized the item he was holding. *The navigation kill switch.*

Her mouth went dry, but she recovered quickly. And bluffed. "What's that?"

Fire burned in his dark eyes. "You know damn well what it is." He took a step toward her, his large body filling her field of view. "Explain yourself."

Fear and anger waged war in her chest, sending her pulse into the stratosphere. "I don't have to explain anything to you."

"*The hell you don't!*" His roar echoed in the enclosed space. "What kind of two-faced con are you running?"

That did it. Her control snapped. "*Me?!*" Her body shook with the effort of keeping her fisted hands at her sides. "What about *you?*"

He jerked like she'd taken a swing at him. "I'm not conning you."

Her anger gained momentum. "Of course you're not. A *mercenary* would never think of stabbing someone in the back."

His brows snapped down. "You're one to talk. I offered you a job!"

"You didn't *offer* me anything! You want to take my ship and make me your slave."

He stared at her. "Have you lost your mind?"

"Maybe. But you've lost your soul."

He growled, looking like a tiger about to pounce. "Careful, Natasha."

"Or what? You'll lock me up? Beat me? Kill me?"

He advanced on her, the ferocity in his gaze making her tremble. "Is that the kind of monster you think I am?"

She backed up, but misjudged the distance. Rather than reaching the hatch, her shoulder blades bumped against the bulkhead, halting her retreat. She lifted her chin, refusing to be cowed. "I think you'll do whatever it takes to get what you want."

He planted his palms on either side of her torso, caging her in. "You don't know what I want."

"You want this ship."

"That, too."

This close, his breath brushed her face. She didn't dare look away, but she was intensely aware of the wall of muscle surrounding her. He could subdue her so easily. She'd seen how he'd handled Shash, who was larger and stronger than she was. But no matter what he did, she wouldn't go down without a fight.

He didn't touch her. They remained frozen, centimeters apart, the heat of anger in his eyes slowly changing to... something else.

A small groove appeared between his brows. "I'm not your enemy."

She swallowed, her tongue darting out to moisten her dry lips.

His gaze followed the motion before his attention returned to her eyes.

Her heart stuttered. Was he—

A sharp trill shattered the silence.

Isin shoved away from the wall and pulled his comm device out of his pocket. "Isin."

A cultured woman's voice responded. "We've identified a Federal patrol ship headed your way."

Isin swore. "Do they know we're here?"

"Unclear. Sweep's attempting to intercept their communications."

"Have Byrd stand by with the *Dagger*."

"Aye."

He met Nat's gaze. "Tell Stevens to shut everything down." Without waiting for a response, he turned to the tactical console and began powering it off.

Nat tapped her comband, her gaze drifting to the kill switch now sitting beside Isin's hand. "Pete?"

"Yeah, Nat?"

"A Fed patrol is on its way. We need to cut power to all systems."

His tone made a U-turn from cheerful to serious. "Done."

Within seconds, the overhead lights went out, plunging them into darkness. Nat turned on the light from her comband, letting out a startled yelp when it revealed Isin's dark shape right beside her. Her comm pinged a moment later. She opened the channel.

"What the hell is going on?" Marlin sounded either frustrated or scared—maybe both.

"We had to cut power. A Fed patrol is on its way."

The strength bled out of his indignation. "Do they know where we are?"

"We don't know. Maybe."

"They must, if they're coming out here."

Isin frowned. "Not necessarily. We aren't the only ones who've used this part of Troi for smuggling activities."

He had a point. She'd begun to think of the ship as an insulated space, detached from the rest of the world. But Troi was a big planet, with a significant amount of traffic on and off world. The presence of this patrol could be totally unrelated to them.

"What do we do?" Marlin asked.

"Sit tight. Isin's ship is tracking the patrol and attempting to access their communications. I'll keep you posted." She closed the channel, not wanting to get drawn into one of Marlin's worry loops.

But that left her with nothing to do except deal with the man standing much too close for comfort.

Stepping around him, she settled into the navigation chair and faced the dark bridgescreen. "Do you think they'll find us?"

He glanced at the ceiling before meeting her gaze. "Probably not. This ship has been hidden for years. Whatever their reasons for coming out here, it's unlikely they'll be looking for anything buried in the sand."

"Right." But his words didn't calm the butterflies dancing around in her stomach. The Feds might find *Gypsy*. She was concealed, but certainly not buried. Last time Nat had checked on her, the sand that had collected on top of the sheets was only a quarter of a meter thick. "What if they–"

Isin's comm trilled again. He opened the channel. "Go ahead."

The same woman spoke without preamble. "They're making a high altitude pass. No indication they're focusing on your location, but they've slowed and their flight path indicates a search pattern."

The lines of tension around Isin's mouth tightened. "How soon until they're overhead?"

"Three minutes."

"Keep the channel open until they've passed us. Alert me to any changes in the pattern."

"Aye."

Isin set the device on the console and settled into the tactical chair.

Nat dropped her voice to a whisper. "Who is that?"

"Itorye. My first mate."

Nat bit down on her tongue to keep from voicing the words that sprang to mind. The cultured voice belonged to the woman Isin was colluding with to hoodwink her. She sounded like someone capable of deception, and more refined than Shash.

They waited in silence, their breathing the only sound in the room.

Itorye's voice came over the line. "Patrol approaching your position."

Nat gripped the armrests. If the Feds found them, things were going to get ugly. They'd lose the ship, for starters. And possibly get locked up for running an illegal salvage operation.

Her gaze fell on Isin. Correction. *She* might get locked up. Isin had a ship on standby. His crew would get him out, one way or another.

She couldn't actually hear the drone of the patrol ship as it passed overhead, but she felt like she could anyway. She held her breath. *One thousand-one, one thousand-two, one thousand-three.*

She got to twelve before Itorye's voice came back over the line. "The patrol is continuing on."

Nat exhaled, allowing her head to fall forward.

Isin picked up his comm device. "Monitor them and alert me to any changes."

"Aye."

He closed the channel, his focus shifting to Nat. "That was exciting."

She grimaced at his deadpan delivery. "I don't consider potential incarceration by Feds exciting."

"I wasn't talking about the Feds." His gaze flicked to the kill switch. "We have a situation."

She couldn't read the look in his eyes. But he didn't seem angry anymore. "Yes, we do."

"Am I correct that this isn't the only device you installed?"

She didn't answer.

"I'll take that as a yes. So, you were planning to hold this ship hostage, is that it?"

She scowled. "You didn't give me a choice."

He blew out a breath, his brows drawing down as he studied her. "What do you mean?"

He seemed genuinely puzzled, which confused the hell out of her. She was good at spotting liars and con artists, especially when she had their number. But if he had any tells, he was hiding them well. "I overheard Shash and Kenji discussing your plan."

"What plan?"

"You know what plan."

"No, I don't."

Now he was just messing with her. She fixed him with a withering look.

But rather than getting upset, he sighed. Pushing out of his seat, he knelt in front of her.

She scrambled as far back as her chair would allow.

He held up his hands, palms out. "Natasha, stop. I'm not going to hurt you."

She stilled. Either he was the best actor she'd ever met, or her reaction was upsetting him. She drew in a slow breath. "Maybe not now. But you will. You're planning to force me to join your crew."

"What?" He grasped the arms of her chair, turning it so they faced each other. "Natasha, no. I *want* you on my crew. I won't deny that. But I would never force you to do anything you don't want to do."

Conflicting facts buzzed like hornets in her brain. "But Shash and Kenji said..."

"What? What did they say?"

She swallowed. Did she have anything to lose by telling him? Nope. "They said that as soon as my crew finished helping you with the repairs, you were going to press us into service."

His eyes widened.

"*Involuntary* service."

He stared at her for three heartbeats before his face contorted in a snarl and he shoved to his feet. He yanked his comm device from his pocket. "Kenji, get your ass to the bridge now! And bring Shash."

She stared at him. She'd thought she'd seen him angry before. But that was nothing compared to the fury turning his eyes into burning coals.

Kenji sounded equally startled. "Uh... sure. Be right there."

Isin closed the channel and faced Nat. The fire still burned in his eyes, but it wasn't directed at her. "I'll deal with this."

All she could do was nod.

He focused his attention on the hatch. Footsteps pounded up the steps less than a minute later. They must have run all the way from the engine room.

Kenji appeared first, his large body caught in the light from the lantern in his hand. He took one look at Isin and snapped to attention. Shash followed him onto the bridge, but rather than focusing on Isin, her gaze narrowed on Nat. A sneer lifted her lips.

Isin's gaze shifted slowly from one to the other. His voice was chillingly soft. "Would either of you care to explain why Natasha believes we plan to abduct her and her crew?"

Kenji scowled at Shash, who seemed unperturbed by Isin's question. "I didn't say anything to her, Cap."

Nat spoke up. "You didn't have to. I overheard you talking. I was in the access tunnel while you were in the C deck corridor."

Kenji grimaced. "Then it *was* my fault, Cap. I shouldn't have talked about it anywhere she might have overheard."

Isin's hands twitched at his sides, like an old-time gunslinger getting ready for a quick draw. "I'm not asking how she *found out*. I'm asking what lunacy made you think I'd even *consider* such a thing in the first place."

Kenji blinked, his gaze darting from Nat to Isin and back again. "Well, uh... we, I mean, you said she was a good pilot—"

"What I *said* was that she's an amazing pilot and would be a huge asset to the crew. I did *not* say I was going to kidnap her!" Isin roared, the words echoing off the bulkhead.

Kenji flinched.

Shash's expression turned malevolent as she glared at Nat.

Nat stared at the three of them in shock. *Isin was defending her? Again?*

His gaze locked onto his two crewmembers—a tiger watching prey. "If we were on *Vengeance,* you'd both be going a few rounds with me in the Cage."

Kenji tensed, but Shash almost smiled.

What the hell was the cage?

"I don't have that luxury here. For now, I'm—" His comm chirped. "*What?*"

If Itorye was surprised by his tone, her voice didn't indicate it. "The patrol ship is returning to your location."

They all glanced at the ceiling.

"Directly to our location?"

"They appear to be circling the area. Shall I dispatch Byrd with the *Dagger?*"

Isin's grip tightened on the comm. His gaze met Nat's. "Stand by. Let's see what they do." He didn't look worried. He looked resigned, like he was preparing for the inevitable.

The seconds ticked by. Isin's gaze returned to the ceiling, like he was watching the patrol with X-ray vision.

What would he do if the Feds landed? Hide on the ship? Ambush the patrol and kill them?

She shuddered. She had no doubt he could do it. But watching him mow through a ship full of Feds who were just doing their jobs was an experience she would prefer to forego.

Itorye's voice came back on the line. "The ship has changed course and is leaving the area."

The collective exhale was audible.

"Unfortunately, they're also sending an excavation team to your location in the morning."

"An excavation team?" Nat frowned. "How do you know that?"

Itorye sounded amused, the first indication of emotion in her voice. "Sweep tapped into a non-secure communication sent to Sage, requesting an excavation team."

Nat met Isin's gaze. "Could they have noticed *Gypsy?*"

"*Gypsy?*" Itorye asked.

"Her shuttle," Isin clarified. "Their sensors might have picked up strong metallic signatures. It's not buried like this ship."

"They certainly noticed something."

Isin held Nat's gaze. "We need to move the ship."

For once, they were in complete agreement. "Can we do it tonight?"

His gaze swung to Shash. "Can you and Stevens get the main engines online?"

Shash's mouth worked like she was chewing on something nasty and trying not to swallow it. "Maybe."

"I can help." Nat ignored Shash's scathing look. "The navigation console's fixed. If you can finish up tactical so we'll have sensors, I'll work with Shash and Pete on the engine repairs."

A spark of warmth lit his eyes. "All right."

Itorye's voice came over the comm. "Would you like me to send down any of the crew to assist?"

He glanced at the device. "No. We can't risk the *Dagger* being spotted. But be ready to move tonight."

"I'll inform the crew."

He closed the channel.

"Marlin and I can help, too," Kenji said.

Isin's gaze swung to Nat. "It's your call."

She felt as lightheaded as she had during her first solo flight. Everything had changed so quickly. It was exhilarating, but terrifying, too. She turned to Kenji. "Follow me."

Twenty-Two

It's your call.

Isin's comment echoed in Nat's ears as she descended the stairs to D deck, with Kenji and Shash right behind her.

If he was playing her, he was doing a masterful job. If he wasn't—

She shoved the thought aside. They could deal with the future after they'd secured the ship. She tapped her comband. "Marlin, meet me in the engine room. We're moving the ship tonight."

"*Tonight?*"

"That's right. The Feds are sending out an excavation team tomorrow morning. We don't want to be here when they arrive."

"Oh. Uh... I'll be right there."

She glanced over her shoulder at Shash. "Which repairs are critical?"

Shash waited a few beats before responding. "The new flow regulator assembly is still sitting on the deck. Can't take off without it. We haven't restored power to the aft and ventral thrusters, either. Without those, we'll never get out of the sand."

"How much time to install the flow regulator?"

"With five people working? Six, maybe seven hours."

That would eat up most of their daylight. "And the thrusters?"

"Two people could do it in about four."

So they wouldn't finish before nighttime. That was okay. They'd want to move the ship under the cover of darkness, anyway.

She stepped through the hatch to the engine room, her comband beam and Kenji's lantern adding to the light from Pete's lantern. He poked his head around the bulkhead, his brows lifting when he spotted them.

"Pete, get the lights up and all systems online. We've got work to do." She quickly filled him in on the situation.

He didn't seem the least bit concerned with the tight timetable. "We'll get it done."

"Good." His can-do attitude lifted her spirits.

Marlin appeared at the hatch, skirting around Shash to reach Nat's side.

"Marlin, I need you and Kenji to help Shash install the flow regulator."

His face drooped like a basset hound's, his gaze swinging between Shash and Kenji.

"Shash is in charge of the operation, so follow her orders."

That earned her a raised eyebrow from Shash.

"Pete and I will restore power to the thrusters, then assist you with the install. One way or another, we have to take off tonight. Let's get moving."

Three hours and forty-five minutes later, Nat's skin was slick with sweat and grime, but the thruster diagnostics indicated the system was operational.

Pete looked as disheveled as she did. He pressed his palms against the engine room console and studied the readouts. The grunts and cursing from the other side of the room indicated work was progressing on the regulator.

Nat used the sleeve of her tunic to wipe sweat out of her eyes. "I'm going to check on Isin and make sure he doesn't need any help on the bridge. I'll stop by the galley on my way back and bring food and water."

Pete nodded. "We'll be here."

She hurried up the aft stairs and trotted down the A deck corridor, glancing at the outside hatch as she passed. What was she going to do about *Gypsy*? She'd cleared a space in the ship's bay large enough to accommodate the shuttle, but that wasn't the biggest issue. She couldn't pilot *Gypsy* and this ship at the same time, and she couldn't bring the shuttle onboard until the ship was free from the sand.

That left her with a dilemma. To get both ships in the air as quickly and efficiently as possible, she'd have to turn over control of one of them to Kenji. He was the only other pilot onboard. But which one?

She stepped onto the bridge.

Isin was bent over the tactical console, scrolling through diagnostic readouts. He glanced at her. "Problem?"

Was he reading her mind? "We still have several hours before we'll finish installing the flow regulator, but that's the only critical piece. Pete has assured me we'll be able to lift off tonight."

"Good." He went back to reading the diagnostic data.

She peered past him. "Any issues here?"

His gaze flicked briefly to hers. "Calibrating the sensors has proven to be a challenge. The mineral content of the sand is blocking our readings. You may have the same issue with navigation. Can you set our course and track our position manually?"

"I've done it before." Asking the system to set navigation protocols while buried under the sand would be like asking someone to follow a compass reading in a pitch black room. "The trick will be staying clear of populated areas and other ships."

"Not a problem." He didn't sound the least bit concerned.

What a difference a year made. This Isin seemed confident they'd figure out a solution to any issue that arose. A year ago, he would have freaked out.

"Any ideas for a heading?" She certainly hadn't given it any thought.

"Itorye's been working on that. There's an uninhabited mountain region to the north. It should be warm enough this time of year to work outside, and we won't have to worry about patrols."

"That sounds good." She looked over the diagnostic data while she debated how to bring up the topic weighing on her mind.

"Something wrong?"

She glanced at him. "I was thinking about *Gypsy*."

"What about her?"

"I can't fly her and this ship at the same time."

He quirked one brow. "And?"

"And we can't dock *Gypsy* until this ship's in the air."

"Kenji can fly *Gypsy*."

"No." She hadn't known her answer until the word popped out of her mouth. She just couldn't bring herself to turn *Gypsy* over to Kenji. It would feel like a betrayal, choosing this ship over her beloved shuttle. "But I'll have to leave this ship to fly her."

"Okay."

"I won't be here." She sounded like an idiot, but she was struggling to form her question. Or statement. Whatever.

He folded his arms. "What's your point?"

She blew out a breath. There was no getting around it. "If I leave the ship to fly *Gypsy*, what's to stop you from taking off in this ship as soon as it's out of the sand?" There. She'd said it.

He stared at her, his expression unreadable. "You could follow us."

"And if you tried to lose me? I'm betting Kenji's an above-average pilot, with combat training."

His jaw worked. "You'd be right. But that's not the point. Why do you think I'd abandon you?"

"I'm just... concerned. That's why I'm asking." Which begged the question of whether she was going to believe whatever he told her.

Emotion flashed in his eyes. "I'm not going to steal this ship."

She wanted to trust him. And unless she planned to turn *Gypsy* over to Kenji, she didn't have a choice, did she? The Feds would be here in the morning. She was out of time.

Worse case scenario, he'd take off without her. She'd hate him for lying, but she'd suffered far worse in the past year. And he'd just told her where he was heading. This ship still needed a lot of repairs. She'd have time to track them down if it came to that.

She nodded. "Good to know."

He continued to stare at her. "Anything else?"

"No."

"Then I'll join you in the engine room and have Kenji take over here."

She squelched the jab of jealousy that hit her. She'd wanted to be the first person to pilot this ship. But she'd made her choice.

Tonight she would take a leap of faith. It wasn't by choice, which probably explained why she felt like a diver standing at the edge of a cliff, anticipating the long drop to the water below.

Hopefully she wouldn't end up smashed against the rocks.

Twenty-Three

"Are you sure you want to stay on the ship?" Nat's gaze swung between Marlin and Pete. She'd gathered them for a quiet convo before she headed out to free *Gypsy* from her sandy cocoon.

Pete nodded. "I doubt they'll try anythin'. Not while they're focused on the Feds, at least. But if they do, I wanna be here to stop 'em."

Anxiety flared in her chest. "Don't get hurt trying to defend this ship." She didn't want him taking risks on her account.

"I can take care of myself. And you could find us usin' the homin' beacon I tied to your comband."

Her lips parted in surprise. "When did you do that?"

"The night we installed the kill switch. The beacon's still workin'."

Amazing. She'd underestimated his resolve to help her keep this ship. She glanced at Marlin. "And you don't want to come with me, either?" She'd expected him to jump at the chance to get away from Isin's crew, even temporarily.

He wasn't nearly as resolute as Pete, but he didn't seem eager to go with her, either. He avoided her gaze. "Well... the thing is..."

"Yes?"

"Docking in that bay?" He made a face. "It doesn't seem safe."

She lifted her brows. "Are you questioning my piloting skills?"

"No. I'm questioning the wisdom of flying into a bay that wasn't designed to hold a shuttle as large as yours."

"It'll be fine." She'd initially fallen in love with *Gypsy* because of the shuttle's ability to maneuver like a hummingbird. And she certainly preferred the option of docking in flight rather than leaving Kenji at the controls of this ship while she and *Gypsy* tagged along behind.

Marlin took a step back. "I think I'll take my chances here."

"So you'd rather fly with the mercenaries than with me? I think I was just insulted."

He gave her a pointed look. "We already had one wild ride together in your shuttle. I don't need a repeat."

"Hmm." It wasn't remotely the same situation, but she let it go. It would be easier to concentrate on her job without a passenger onboard, anyway. Especially a nervous one. "I'll keep the channel open for my comband. If you want to get in touch with me, use that. I'll need *Gypsy*'s comm for coordinating with Isin."

"No worries." Pete rested a hand on Marlin's shoulder. "We'll be fine, won't we?"

Marlin managed a weak smile. "Yeah. Fine."

"Then I'll see you two after we're in the air."

The outside hatch was already open when she reached it, the stars visible in the inky sky. Climbing out onto the dune, she glanced at the valley where *Gypsy*'s form was illuminated by a light bobbing in the darkness. A faint rustling and a thump reached her as one of the sheets and its accompanying pile of sand slid down the shuttle's flank and dropped onto the ground.

The light swung in her direction as she made her way down the slope. She recognized Isin's vague outline. "I didn't expect you to help me."

"The sooner we get *Gypsy* ready, the sooner we can get out of here." Isin tossed the sandy fabric onto a pile near his feet.

She switched on the light for her comband and moved to the next anchor. "So the ship's ready for takeoff?" Her voice came out remarkably calm considering the knots that were steadily wrapping themselves around her insides. She'd envisioned this moment in a thousand different scenarios during her year of captivity. Now that it was here, her brain was flooding her with all the ways it could go wrong.

"As ready as we can be." Another sheet slid off Gypsy's side, the falling sand creating a plume of dust.

She waved it away from her face. "*Gypsy*'s aerial grenades are going to create quite a show if anyone's watching." She'd calculated the ship had at least a hundred cubic meters of sand burying it beneath the dunes. Her task was to use *Gypsy*'s aerial grenades to blast off the top layers of sand, lightening the load. Once the majority of the ship's dorsal hull had been uncovered, the ship's engines would be able to take over to free it from its sandy tomb and get it airborne.

"Itorye will be monitoring for incoming ships." He acted like he did this type of maneuver every day.

Back when they were on the *Sphinx* together, his self-assurance had mostly been a bluff. She doubted he bluffed anymore.

He reached for the last sheet. "If you can start a landslide, even better."

The sheet slid away, leaving *Gypsy* as bare as a newborn. Nat patted the shuttle's hull. "*Gypsy* and I can handle it."

Isin gave a little snort as he picked up the sheet and rolled it into a loose bundle.

That snort rankled. Either he was questioning her abilities, or he was questioning her friendship with *Gypsy*.

Well, he could stuff a sock in it. Without *Gypsy*, she wouldn't have survived her time with the Setarips. She owed the shuttle her life. And her sanity. If he couldn't understand that, too bad.

She opened the back hatch and stepped inside, her body tingling with anticipation. The familiar confines wrapped around her like a hug.

Isin came up behind her, two huge bundles of sandy sheets in his arms. He dropped them onto the deck, spraying sand everywhere.

She glared.

He just shrugged. "We're short on time. Would you prefer I leave them outside?"

"No." Resources were precious, and that included sandy sheets. She'd just have to set aside time to sweep out *Gypsy* when they reached their destination. She didn't want sand making its way into her bunk.

He nodded toward the cockpit. "Go power up. I'll finish loading the supplies."

He was giving orders again—taking charge and expecting her to follow along.

She could beat him at that game.

She turned away and started for the cockpit. "Close the hatch when you're done."

Twenty-Four

Grabbing her duster off the peg behind the pilot's seat, she slipped it on. She didn't need it for warmth, but wearing it was part of her flying routine, kind of like a good luck charm.

"Ready for a little target practice?" She ran her hand over *Gypsy*'s console after she strapped in. "We'll show them how mighty you are by knocking all that sand away from the big ship."

Talking to *Gypsy* was a habit she'd developed shortly after she'd acquired her, but she rarely indulged when she had traveling companions unless she wanted them to look at her strangely.

She switched on power to the engines. A subtle hum made the back of her chair vibrate. While the engines warmed up, she went through her pre-flight checklist, keeping an eye on the aft camera. Isin emerged into her field of view, carrying the anchors they'd used to secure the sheets in place. He disappeared through the back hatch. A faint clink told her he'd left the items on the deck with the sheets. A moment later a tone from the console confirmed the hatch had sealed.

She switched to the lateral cameras, watching as he climbed the dune until he moved out of sight. She drew in a breath, her stomach dancing around like a kite on a windy day.

The engines completed their warm-up cycle, all systems checking out normal. When the comm pinged, she opened the channel.

"All clear." Isin said. "The ship is secured."

"Lifting off." Nat engaged the ventral thrusters.

Gypsy rose with the grace of a dancer, clearing the dune and giving Nat a view of the surrounding area. She scanned for ships, but nothing showed on sensors. Isin had said Itorye would alert them if that changed. Hopefully he was right, because the task at hand would take all Nat's concentration.

"Scanning the dune." The mineral content made it impossible to get accurate readings below the surface, but that didn't matter. She wanted a 3D image of the dune itself.

When the scan completed, she aligned the image with the blueprint she'd created for the ship using the schematic program on her comband, adjusting for the ship's slight degree of tilt until the two matched up. The resulting composite showed a density map for the quantity of sand surrounding the ship on all sides.

"How does it look?" Isin asked.

"A lot of sand."

He grunted in response.

She identified her first target, calibrating the weapons so that the impact would blast away the sand, not the ship. "First target locked. Preparing to fire."

"Remember we don't have any shielding."

As if she'd forget that important detail. But Isin had never been able to hold his tongue when she was doing her job. In a way, the familiar nagging was comforting. Annoying, but comforting. "I'll be careful."

Turning on the autopilot to hover mode, she double-checked her data and the status of the aerial grenades. Good to go. "Firing."

The first grenade hit in a bright flash. Sand shot fifty meters into the air in a giant geyser, some of it raining down on *Gypsy*'s hull. Nat switched on the shuttle's shields. No reason to take unnecessary damage.

She checked the sand density map. A sizeable hole had been created in the shelf covering the ship's starboard side, exposing the metallic hull in several places. It was a good beginning.

"Any issues?" she asked Isin.

"Nothing we didn't expect. What do you see?"

"The shot exposed part of the hull. Unfortunately, the sand's holding together. I'm moving to the port side."

"Understood."

Maneuvering *Gypsy* into position, she lined up the second shot. "Firing."

Another plume exploded into the air, the granules pelting *Gypsy*'s shields. As the sky cleared, the sand near the blast point shifted, flowing like water away from the hull and down the slope of the dune. The glow from *Gypsy*'s running lights reflected off the long swath of metal the river of sand had revealed, as well as the portholes and viewports lining the exterior of B and C deck.

A squiggle of excitement rippled through Nat's abdomen. She could see her ship! "Starboard side is visible to C deck."

Isin's response held a note of warning. "You need to pick up the pace."

"Why?"

"Two Federal ships are heading our way."

Twenty-Five

Nat swore as she brought up her targeting data. "This might get bumpy."

"Just get us loose."

She guided *Gypsy* into position for her third shot. Checking the readings again, she adjusted her calculations. Now that the ship wasn't as protected by the sand, she had to be precise in her targeting.

"Are you going to fire anytime soon?" Isin growled.

"I'm recalculating. Unless you'd prefer that I just pull the trigger and blow a hole in the hull."

"We don't have time for—"

"You interrupting me? I agree."

His exasperated huff came across the line. She smiled grimly. This version of Isin she knew well.

"Firing."

She pulled *Gypsy* to the starboard side as soon as the grenade was away, targeting the next shot as the debris from the previous one rained down. The two port shots had jostled some sand on this side, too, but most of the ship was still covered. She didn't take time to double-check her calculations on this one. "Firing."

The flash and boom that followed triggered the avalanche she'd wanted. A huge section of sand calved away, revealing the broadside of the ship in all its glory, right down to D deck. She could even see a section of the aft engine.

"You're cleared to D deck."

"Firing aft and ventral thrusters."

She backed *Gypsy* off as an orange glow bloomed to the aft of the ship, turning the dune into a maelstrom of churning sand. The power of the thrusters drove the ship out of its terrestrial prison, sand cascading down the hull in curtains as the ship rose into the sky like a phoenix from the ashes. It cleared the dune and banked in her direction. They'd done it! Her ship was free.

A chime sounded on *Gypsy*'s console, drawing Nat's attention. A flashing light on her comm console indicated an incoming hail. She switched the channel to answer the hail.

A woman's clipped voice filled the cockpit. "Shuttle pilot, this is Federal Patrol Alpha. We have you on sensors. Land your craft immediately and prepare to be boarded."

Did that order ever produce the desired result? "I'm sorry, now's not convenient. Maybe later." She switched the channel back over to Isin. "Just heard from the Feds."

"Same here. Get ready for docking."

"I can't dock now." The ship would be vulnerable while the bay door was open. And the procedure would take time. Her priority was escaping the Feds. She had to convince Isin to run.

"What do you mean you can't dock?"

"I'm heading for the mountains." She changed course and pushed *Gypsy*'s engines, running perpendicular to the path of the approaching patrol ships as they appeared on her display. The incoming hail light on the comm panel continued to blink. She ignored it. "Take off. I'll draw both ships if I can."

Dead silence for a heartbeat. "I'm not leaving you."

"Isin, go. I'll catch up with you later." The mountains were coming closer. She'd maneuvered *Gypsy* through those mountains before. She could do it again.

Movement to starboard made her turn her head. Her ship had drawn alongside *Gypsy*, like two sprinters racing to the finish line. She bared her teeth. "Isin, don't be an idiot! The ship's barely functional and you don't have any shields or weapons. You have to go!"

"Like hell! Dock and we'll—"

"No! I can lose them. I'll be fine. Just—"

"Get into position! We're running out—"

"I'll make—"

"*Natasha!*" His roar echoed in the cockpit, startling her into silence. "Dock the shuttle now or so help me I'll knock *Gypsy* out of the sky!"

She stared at the speaker. He sounded completely serious.

She made her decision in a millisecond. "Open the bay doors."

Twenty-Six

Nat muttered a litany of swear words as she brought *Gypsy* in line with the opening to the bay. After this was over, she and Isin were going to have a little talk about his attitude.

The edge of the mountains streaked past in her peripheral vision, the ship's glowing engines creating ribbons of heat in the dry air in front of her. She and Kenji had altered course to run parallel to the mountain range, trying to maintain their distance from the patrol ships, but her sensors told her they were losing ground every second.

The lights in the bay created a rectangular target in the surrounding darkness. While she'd completed this type of inflight docking maneuver plenty of times, she'd never flown into this particular bay. The presence of the patrol ships and the debris cluttering half the bay certainly wasn't making her job easier.

She steadily closed the gap, the rectangle growing larger, the ship's interior lights casting shadows in the shuttle's cockpit. At ten meters out, she dropped *Gypsy's* shields and lowered the landing gear, nudging the shuttle forward until the bay doors slipped past her peripheral vision. The shuttle's stabilizers kicked in as the wind resistance changed. She lowered *Gypsy* toward the deck. A couple meters more and—

"Weapons fire!"

The blare of the bay's security alarms drowned out Isin's shout. A bright light flashed and her view of the cargo bay tilted laterally by forty degrees. The scrape of metal on metal preceded a loud bang that rattled Nat's teeth as the deck smacked into *Gypsy*.

She cut the engines and braced for impact. *Gypsy* slid along the deck, ramming into the portside bulkhead with a crunch.

The harness kept her in her chair, the straps digging into her torso. Another jolt flung her sideways. "Isin! What the hell—"

"Are you okay?" he barked.

"I'm not dead."

"Get up here!"

She craned her neck around. The cargo bay door was already closing, but she caught a flash of movement from outside. The patrol ships had caught up with them. And they weren't playing nice.

She unfastened her harness, but instantly regretted it when the ship lurched, flinging her out of her chair. The shuttle scraped across the deck, the high-pitched whine hurting her ears. The bay had docking clamps, but they were useless in this situation. She slapped the button to magnetize Gypsy's landing gear.

The screech of metal abruptly ceased as *Gypsy* jerked to a halt. Thank goodness. She didn't relish the idea of being crushed by her own shuttle.

She hurried to the shuttle's back hatch, which moaned in protest as it descended, one corner clanking down while the other remained half a meter in the air. She hopped to the deck, peering under the shuttle's belly. One of the landing struts was mangled, but still had enough contact to maintain the magnetic hold. Isin would pay for that repair, and any other damage *Gypsy* had sustained. But she'd deal with that later.

She braced her hand on *Gypsy*'s side as the deck bucked beneath her feet. "Gotta go. girl. Lunatic on the bridge."

Twenty-Seven

Focusing on a point on the bulkhead to steady herself, she sprinted across the deck, touching down as lightly as possible to keep the ship's uneven motion from throwing her off balance. The stairs were a fun adventure, her arms pinwheeling as she fought to stay on her feet. Grabbing onto the railing, she used brute strength to reach the exit.

Navigating the corridors was easier. She kept her arms out to her sides and pushed off the bulkheads whenever the ship's motion pitched her off center. Either the ship's stabilizers weren't working, or Kenji hadn't turned them on.

The stairway up to A deck presented another obstacle. The ship continued to pitch and jerk like it was caught in the hands of an angry child. She slammed her elbow into the bulkhead navigating from C to B deck, and her shoulder took a hit halfway to A deck. By the time she made it to the bridge, her breath was blowing in and out like a bellows.

She grabbed onto the frame of the hatch. Alarms blared from the tactical console and a blinking light indicated an incoming comm message.

Isin sat hunkered at tactical, his lips pulled back in a sneer. "Mangy, soul-sucking, worm—"

"Talking about me?" Nat asked, shoving off and using the captain's chair for balance as the ship shimmied.

He glanced at her in surprise. "That was quick."

"I flew."

"Kenji, take over tactical." He motioned to Kenji to vacate the pilot's seat while he stood and moved next to Nat.

Kenji set the autopilot before relinquishing the controls.

Isin propelled Nat into the pilot's seat, gripping the back of her chair as she strapped in.

"Are you okay?" he asked.

"Relatively." They'd talk later about the damage to her shuttle.

She glanced at the display. The two patrol ships were dogging their backside but were no longer gaining on them. Kenji had kept the ship out over the dunes while she'd docked rather than seeking cover in the mountains. She adjusted course, heading toward the dark range.

Isin loomed over her. "This isn't *Gypsy*. You can't maneuver this ship in those canyons."

"Watch me." One look at the ship's exterior had confirmed what she'd suspected—it was designed for terrestrial flight as much as space flight. It would fly like a bird on the wing. Assuming everything held together.

She skimmed closer to the ground to avoid a barrage from the leading ship. "We can't keep taking this kind of damage."

"We won't have to. Kenji'll have the cannons firing in less than a minute."

She shot him an incredulous look. "They're operational?" She hadn't even known Kenji had restored functionality to the weapons.

"You weren't the only one pulling late nights. Shash and Stevens are working on the shields. And *Vengeance* will be here in five minutes."

Her stomach muscles clenched. If *Vengeance* joined the fight, that would spell disaster for the patrol ships. A month ago she wouldn't have cared. But her time with the *Starhawke* crew had changed her perspective. The Feds were doing their jobs, enforcing the law and protecting the residents. They weren't evil. And while she certainly didn't want them to get her ship, she didn't intend to kill anyone, either. Not if there was another way.

She motioned to the blinking comm signal. "Are you going to answer that?"

"No point."

The controls jerked in her hand as the ship took another hit. She banked to the right, lining up with an opening in the peaks ahead. "Why not?"

"They've already said the pertinent part. *Land the ship and prepare to be boarded.*"

"So what? You're a negotiator. Negotiate."

"I *don't* negotiate. Not anymore."

The cold decisiveness in his voice made her shiver. "They're Feds, Isin, not mercenaries. They're doing their jobs. *We're* the ones breaking the law." And she had no problem with that. She just didn't want innocent people to pay the price.

"Why do you care what happens to them?"

She briefly met his gaze. "I don't want more blood on my hands."

His expression closed down as he turned to Kenji. "How long on those cannons?"

"Fifteen seconds."

Great. Instead of altering his decision, she'd solidified it. "We don't need the weapons." She had to change his mind. "I can outmaneuver them." They were almost to the mountains.

"Not if they take us out first."

A new warning light flashed on the console. The engines were overheating. She switched on the comm to the engine room. "Pete? What's wrong with the engines?"

He sounded harried. "What's wrong is this ship ain't flown in years, and you're makin' her go like a bat outta hell."

"Can't be helped. Any luck with those shields?"

"Shash needs another minute."

"We don't have a minute." She turned to Isin. "Strap in."

He glared, but moved to the captain's chair and fastened the harness.

"Hold on," she told Pete. "This is gonna get bumpy."

The weapons fire from the patrol ships increased as she guided the ship between the first two mountain peaks. Another alarm went off, indicating a hull fracture. Good thing they weren't leaving atmo.

"Cannons online," Kenji called out.

"Fire," Isin said before Nat could react.

"No!" But she was too late. Cannon fire streaked out, smashing into the patrol ships' shields, making them flare in the aft camera view. "Kenji, don't—"

"Aim for their weapons, not critical systems," Isin said to Kenji.

The patrol ships changed formation to evade the next set of blasts.

"But you better have a plan, Natasha. We can't keep wasting ammo, and *Vengeance* will take care of this problem if we don't."

His implication was clear. His crew wouldn't hesitate to destroy the patrol ships.

There had to be a way out of this that wouldn't involve bloodshed. And that wouldn't burn out the ship's engines. If only there was a way to keep *Vengeance* from—

An idea popped into her head. "*Vengeance* is a warship, right?"

"Of course. Why?"

"How big?" She banked into a side canyon as weapons fire from the patrol ships lit up the rock face to port. The starboard wing barely missed clipping the corner. Isin was right—the ship didn't maneuver like *Gypsy*. At least, not yet. But it had a lot lighter touch than most ships its size.

Kenji sent a return volley.

"How big is *Vengeance*?" she repeated.

"Almost twice this ship's size."

Even better. "Contact Itorye. Tell her to meet us at these coordinates." She rattled them off.

"What are you—"

"Just do it, Isin!" She dropped them low as one of the ships sent a torpedo their way. It sailed overhead and crashed into the canyon wall, sending a shower of boulders spraying into the chasm. She dodged them, skimming close to the opposite wall.

The Feds were getting serious. That was fine. So was she.

The light for the external comm lit up. "Itorye, change course." Isin repeated Nat's coordinates.

"We'll have to break visual on your position," Itorye replied.

"I'm aware." But he didn't question Nat's orders.

Good thing she'd spent some time exploring the area surrounding her former campsite. "When you get there, fly low down the center of the canyon. We'll meet you there shortly."

"Captain?"

"Do as she says."

"Aye."

Isin left the comm channel open, but directed his question to Nat. "What's your plan?"

The blasts from her ship's cannons struck the canyon walls, forcing the Feds to slow down to avoid falling debris.

"*We* can't leave the planet. But *Vengeance* can."

"Why would *Vengeance*–" He paused. "You're going to get them to go after *Vengeance* instead?"

"Yep."

"Why wouldn't they follow us both?"

"Because they're going to think we're in pieces." The patrol ships had slowed down considerably since entering the canyons. The pilots didn't seem as comfortable flying in the tight quarters as she was. And the same mineral content in the sand was affecting sensor readings here, too. If the patrol ships lost visual, they wouldn't be able to track her ship.

She checked the aft camera, catching a glimpse of one of the ships before the curve of the rocks blocked them out. They were almost out of visual range. But that wouldn't last, either. One of the Fed ships would decide to go high to gain speed and tag team with the one staying on her tail. She needed to reach *Vengeance* before that happened. "Itorye, what's your current position?"

"Five kilometers from the coordinates you gave me."

She glanced at Kenji. "Pull up the navigation chart and enter their exact position and speed."

Isin spoke with Itorye as Nat took the ship through a series of weaving turns. Marlin had complained she was flying too fast the last time she'd taken him along this route.

She hadn't mentioned she was doing half speed to keep him from freaking out.

The navigation information populated her display. Perfect. "Itorye, we're about to intersect your position from a side canyon. Slow as much as you can and have weapons ready. As soon as we drop a load of debris, blast it with everything you've got."

"Understood." If Itorye thought the order was strange, she didn't indicate it.

"What debris?" Isin asked.

"In the bay. When I made room for *Gypsy*, I netted everything I'd cleared, and secured it against three of the exterior cargo doors." She'd planned to go through it to see if anything was salvageable. But their immediate need nixed that possibility.

"You're going to dump it?"

"That's right."

Nat guided the ship around a curve, sweeping into the main canyon with the river tumbling along the center. The glow of *Vengeance*'s engines up ahead made her heart thump in anticipation. She hit the throttle, streaking over the top of the larger ship. She triggered the command to open the three cargo doors and adjusted the ship's attitude, letting gravity do the rest. "Cargo away!"

She increased throttle and peeled the ship off into a side canyon.

A massive explosion lit up the aft view, flaming debris scattering before darkness closed in again as they followed the curve of the canyon. She cut the engines to quarter power and glided as close to the ground as she dared.

"The patrol ships are engaging *Vengeance*," Itorye informed them.

"Return fire." Isin replied.

"Isin—" Nat protested, glancing over her shoulder.

He silenced her with a raised hand. "But aim to disable, not destroy. If you blow up either ship, you'll answer to me."

"Understood."

"Stay in the canyon as long as you can, then go for launch. We'll notify you when we're clear."

"Acknowledged."

Would Isin's crew follow his orders? Or would they destroy the patrol ships?

He seemed to read her mind. "Itorye will handle it."

She chose to believe him, because she didn't have a choice. "Okay." Releasing her breath, she nudged the throttle forward, picking up speed and guiding the ship toward the edge of the mountain range.

They reached an open stretch of ground to the north, leading to another mountain range in the distance. She glanced at Kenji. "I'm not seeing anything on sensors."

He studied the display. "Neither am I, but it only takes one."

"Then keep your eyes open."

He shot her a look. "Always."

That look said so much.

She cleared her throat. "Do we have a heading?"

"Itorye sent a route that will allow us to reach our new landing site without passing any habitable areas." Kenji sent the information to her display.

She looked it over. "Seems reasonable." And they could make it in a few hours at their present speed.

The internal comm chimed. "Nat, you got a minute?"

"Go ahead, Pete."

"We got damage to the injectors we put in this mornin'. Didn't break 'em in proper, so they overheated. They need repairs."

"Can it wait until we reach our destination?"

"How far?"

"Sixteen-hundred kilometers."

"No, ma'am. If you wanna stay in the air more'n fifteen minutes, we gotta switch to auxiliary and take the main system offline."

"But we can keep flying?"

"For now. But auxiliary's not as strong. It'll slow you down to 'bout quarter of current speed."

That had just quadrupled her time estimate. She was going to be flying all night and into the morning.

When they reached the edge of the next mountain range, Nat kept the ship close to the ground, following the natural curve of the foothills as she slowed. "Switching to auxiliary engines."

The ship gave a little hiccup, bouncing her in her chair. She gripped the controls, but it smoothed out. "Okay, Pete. You should be good to go."

"On it."

Nat rolled her shoulders to release some of the tension that had gathered there.

"Kenji can take over for a while."

She glanced at Isin. He was watching her, a frown pulling his lips into a reverse bow. Kenji had a similar expression on his face. Too bad for them. She wasn't going anywhere. "That's okay."

Isin's frown deepened. "It's a long way."

"And I'll be fine."

A line appeared between his brows, but eventually he rose from the captain's chair and motioned to Kenji. "Then we'll see what we can do to help with repairs."

"Take a look at *Gypsy.*"

He paused with one hand on the hatch frame. "*Gypsy?*"

"She got banged up during docking."

The frown reappeared. "Then we'll start there. Alert me if you have any issues. Or want a break."

She nodded, turning back to the bridgescreen. "I will."

But she didn't expect to take any breaks. She was finally at the helm of her ship. If this was a dream, she didn't want to ever wake up.

Twenty-Eight

Nat hadn't flown at such a leisurely pace in—come
to think of it, she'd *never* flown at such a leisurely pace.
Although it was far from relaxing. She kept a close eye on
the sensor readings, watching for any tick that might
indicate approaching ships.

Footsteps padded up the stairway, the tread too
light to be Isin or Kenji. She glanced over her shoulder as
Marlin poked his head through the hatch.

"Mind if I join you?"

"Not at all." She welcomed the company. Two sets
of eyes were better than one. "But I might put you to work
watching the sensors."

"That's fine." He placed a container on the
navigation console before settling into the tactical chair.
"Thought you might be hungry."

Her stomach grumbled on cue. "Guess I am. Thanks."
She switched on the autopilot and pulled the lid off the
container, inhaling the aromas of a hearty vegetable stew.
She slid a set of utensils out of their holder in the lid and
dug in. "You just made this?"

He shook his head. "This is from a big batch I made
yesterday and put in the freezer. I re-heated it."

"It's delicious. Thank you."

"You're welcome." His gaze shifted to the
bridgescreen. They were still on the night side of the planet,
so there wasn't much to see except starlight and the tops of
the trees. "No more sand."

"Just what we brought with us." They'd be cleaning it out of their clothes and the deck for a while.

He nodded, but his face looked pinched. Something was bothering him.

She put the lid back on the container and set it on the console, pivoting to face him. "What's on your mind, Marlin?"

He glanced at her. "I'm just wondering what happens now."

"You mean, now on this flight, or now in the future?"

"I mean now with this ship. Isin's other ship and crew are out there somewhere." He gestured to the bridgescreen. "I assume they'll be dropping in soon. Do you think they'll..." He trailed off with a half-hearted shrug.

She tried for levity. "Make us walk the plank?"

He didn't bite. "Something like that."

She wanted to reassure him, but she didn't know the answer. Her gaze swept the bridge and she sighed. "Isin offered me a job."

"He did?"

"All of us, actually. I'd be captain and pilot of this ship, operating under his command, and you and Pete would be part of my crew."

"And he'd pay us?"

"That's what he said."

"Do you believe him?"

"Maybe." He'd certainly seemed sincere when he'd laid into Kenji and Shash. "I don't know."

"Would you do it? Take the job?"

"I—" She frowned. "I don't know the answer to that, either. The whole point of getting this ship was gaining my freedom—not working for someone else, or being subjected to their whims. If I don't fight now, I might never get another chance." The odds of stumbling across a second derelict vessel, or earning enough money to buy a ship, were a trillion to one.

"But if you fight, you're taking on a bunch of mercenaries."

"Uh-huh." Even if she convinced Isin to give her the ship, he'd implied his crew might mutiny. She had no idea how she'd deal with that possibility.

"Are you still thinking of stealing the ship?"

A squiggle of unease wound through her tummy. Stealing the ship now, after they'd all worked together to escape the Feds, just felt... wrong. Like a betrayal. Which was ludicrous. She'd stolen things all her life. Why was she having doubts now? "I'm not sure. Either way, I need a plan."

"Don't we all." He sounded wistful.

She blew out a breath. "I'm really sorry, Marlin. I thought this would be an easy job. I wouldn't have roped you in if I'd anticipated this scenario." She'd wanted to offer him a better situation than he would have had on his own. Instead, he was dealing with mercenaries and at loose ends regarding his future.

"Not your fault."

"Feels like it."

He shrugged. "It's just... life."

And didn't that sum it up. "If I decided to accept Isin's offer, would you stay on with me? If it meant we'd be working for mercenaries?"

He stared at the bridgescreen. "It's not the mercenaries that bother me."

"Oh?" She'd thought it was absolutely the mercenaries that bothered him.

"It's what they do."

"Ah." They were in agreement on that point. And it was something she'd have to consider carefully before making any decisions. Working for Isin didn't seem like the worst option in the world, but piloting a crew full of guns for hire who fought for whoever had the deepest pockets— the very idea made her gut clench.

The vision she had for her future was about building something she could be proud of, not becoming the captain of a ship that left a trail of death and destruction in its wake.

Twenty-Nine

"Make a pass over that plateau." Isin pointed to a rocky stretch of ground covered in patches of snow and scrub grass.

Nat took the ship in a slow arc that gave them a good view of the site from all sides. "We certainly wouldn't have to worry about the ship sinking."

She'd meant it as a serious comment, but Isin gave her a withering look. She stuck her tongue out at him. "What? Rocky is good. You wouldn't want to set down next to that lake we passed a few minutes ago. The mud would lock onto the ship better than docking clamps."

He continued as if she hadn't spoken. "The landing supports should be able to handle the uneven terrain. And the mountains provide good cover. A ship would have to fly directly overhead to spot us."

"What about *Vengeance*? Is there enough room for both ships?"

"Doesn't matter."

She glanced at him. "It doesn't? Aren't they going to come help us with the repairs?"

"No. I told Itorye to keep the ship out of the system. We don't want to stir up the Feds again, or lead them to our location. After the chase *Vengeance* took them on, they'll be monitoring incoming traffic a lot more closely."

"So we're on our own?"

"For now."

Some of the tension eased from her shoulders. She wouldn't have to deal with the rest of Isin's crew just yet. "Then let's set down so we can get started."

She'd anticipated an awkward landing considering the rocky terrain, but the landing gear settled onto the surface with nary a bump. Whoever had designed this ship had clearly been focused on the comfort of the passengers and making their journey as pleasant as possible.

Powering down the engines released even more tension. They'd made it. And the ship was still in one piece.

As sunlight flowed in through the bridgescreen in a warm glow, the full impact of that realization sunk in.

They'd made it!

She could see the entire bridge without artificial lighting because the bridgescreen was no longer blocked with sand. They'd achieved their goal. The ship was free.

She glanced at Isin.

He was watching her. "You okay?" A furrow pinched his brows.

"Yeah. Just taking it all in."

His expression cleared. He stood and gestured to the hatch. "Ready to take a look from the outside?" His dark eyes seemed luminous in the early morning light.

She'd never seen him looking so... chipper. "Absolutely."

He opened a ship-wide comm channel. "Anyone who'd like to get some fresh air, meet us in the bay in five minutes."

They descended the stairs to C deck and continued along the passageway toward the aft. The sunlight flooding in through the viewports stopped her in her tracks. It was like she was seeing the ship for the first time. Beautiful didn't begin to cover it.

But when they stepped onto the catwalk overlooking the bay, she sucked in a breath. "Oh, *Gypsy*."

Last night she'd been so intent on getting to the bridge she'd only taken a cursory glance at her shuttle. From this vantage point, she got a bird's eye view of the damage as she descended the stairs to the deck. The poor shuttle looked like she'd gone ten rounds with an angry rhino.

In addition to the crippled landing strut, the left wing was bent, and she had a dent on her side where she'd collided with the bulkhead.

Nothing Nat couldn't fix, but she hated seeing her friend battered and bruised, especially after she'd just gotten cleaned up and restored while they were on the *Starhawke*.

The bay had taken its licks, too. The paint flakes and scratches on the deck matched the ones on *Gypsy*'s undercarriage, and the bulkhead had a few new indentations where the shuttle had made contact.

Nat rested a hand on the shuttle's side. "Don't you worry, girl. I'll make you good as new."

"I'll help."

Nat turned.

Isin stood with his feet braced apart, surveying the shuttle. "If you want me to."

His offer surprised her. "You will?" She'd assumed he'd be focused on repairing the ship.

He nodded. "I told you to dock. This is my fault."

If she hadn't been leaning against *Gypsy*, she would have fallen over. Isin was accepting blame?

"After we finish clearing the bay to better accommodate her, we can sketch out potential modifications to make it easier to dock in flight."

Her mouth hinged open. She snapped it shut. "That'll be expensive."

Isin held her gaze. "She's worth it."

Nat got the distinct impression he wasn't talking about the shuttle. The intense look she'd seen in his eyes the previous day was back. "I—"

"I thought we were getting off this bucket." Shash's brash voice cut through the moment like a scythe as she and the rest of the crew descended the stairs.

Isin's brows lifted. He pointed to the control panel on the wall. "Be my guest."

Shash stalked past them, but not before shooting Nat a dirty look. Kenji ambled over from the staircase at a more leisurely pace, with Marlin and Pete bringing up the rear.

The air servos hissed as the bay doors parted and the ramp extended, allowing a river of sunshine and crisp morning air to flow into the bay.

Marlin barked in surprise, wrapping his arms around his torso. "It's *freezing* out there!"

Kenji stared down at him. "What did you expect? We're in the mountains."

"I *know* we're in the mountains." Marlin's lips pursed as he rubbed his hands up and down his arms. "But this is arctic."

Kenji let out an amused snort. "We're gonna need to toughen you up, little man." He slapped a palm against Marlin's shoulder and left it there, marching him down the ramp in the direction Shash had disappeared.

Marlin looked too startled to resist.

Pete joined Isin and Nat, his thumbs hooked into the pockets of his pants. "Good flyin' last night."

"Thanks. And thanks for keeping us in the air."

"You bet."

She glanced at Isin. He hadn't followed Shash or Kenji down the ramp. He appeared to be waiting for her. "Shall we?"

"After you."

She strode out into the sunshine, Pete on one side and Isin on the other. Her duster kept the chill from penetrating, but it wouldn't have mattered. She'd spent so much of her life in adverse conditions that she wasn't the least bit temperature sensitive.

Besides, she had better things to think about. Like her ship.

Watching it rise from the sand last night had thrilled her to her toes, but she hadn't been able to enjoy the moment thanks to the arrival of the Feds. Now she was getting her first good look at the vessel that had given her a purpose during the long, dark days of her captivity.

She hadn't expected the hull to be painted, since the hatch and surrounding areas had been bare metal, but looking at the ship now, it was clear the swirling winds had sandblasted the paint off. The lower two-thirds of the ship didn't match the gunmetal grey of the top. It was painted a muted gold that glimmered in the morning light.

"What do you think?" Pete stood beside her, surveying the ship. "Is it what you pictured?"

Her breath came out on a sigh. "Better. Way better."

"Yep. She's pretty."

"It's a hunk of metal with an engine," Shash retorted, turning her back to the ship and glaring at Nat. "A banged up one at that."

Isin moved to Nat's other side, placing himself between her and Shash. "You'll have to forgive Shash. She has trouble admitting sentimentality or affection for objects. Or people, for that matter."

Shash's glare shifted to him. "Says the pot to the kettle."

He stared her down.

She huffed, moving off to join Kenji and Marlin as they circled the ship.

Pete leaned toward Nat. "Don't mind her," he said in an undertone. "She likes this ship more than she's lettin' on."

"Oh?" Nat didn't consider that good news. If Shash didn't like the ship, she'd be more inclined to return to *Vengeance.* That would suit Nat just fine.

"Yep. She was gettin' downright excited last night, talkin' about makin' engine modifications to boost speed."

Nat grimaced. "I have trouble picturing her getting excited about anything."

Pete shrugged. "Some folks are wired different."

And some folks were wired badly.

"There's not as much damage to the hull as I'd expected." Nat started circling the ship in the opposite direction Shash had taken.

Isin followed her. "From the initial crash? Or the weapons fire?"

"The crash." The scorch marks on the paint gave testament to the blows the Feds had landed. "The shields must have held during the initial impact." The belly of the ship seemed to have taken the brunt of the impact when the ship had plowed into the dune, indicating the pilot had been able to keep the ship level during the approach.

"Makes sense," Pete replied. "Shields and weapons on this ship have an independent power source from engines and navigation. The surge didn't knock them out."

Nat bent her head as pressure built behind her eyes. If the engine failure and resulting gaseous leak hadn't pushed lethal toxins into the ship's circulation system, the crew might have survived.

Until now, she'd been able to push aside the role their deaths had played in saving her life, in helping her to reach for a brighter future. She owed so much to a group of people who'd died when she was still a teenager. She and Isin both did. He'd buried their bodies, his way of showing respect for their loss and sacrifice. She needed to come up with her own method for honoring them.

Isin's shadow blocked the sun. "Problem?"

She met his gaze. "No. Just thinking." She called out to Pete, who was standing near one of the landing supports, examining the impact damage to the hull. "What's your time estimate for making her spaceworthy?"

He cocked his head, assessing. "Assumin' we can manufacture any parts we need? Two weeks."

Two weeks? She glanced at Isin.

He seemed as surprised by the estimate as she was. "That's all?"

Pete nodded. "Shash and I'll do a thorough check of course, but the hull looks sturdy."

She'd expected to have a month or more to consider her options. Two weeks felt way too close for comfort.

Isin's gaze met hers. She saw a similar uneasiness in his eyes. Was he dreading their showdown when he insisted on keeping the ship? Or bracing for a mutiny from his crew if he turned the ship over to her?

Either way, the clock was ticking.

Thirty

"I can't believe you painted it red."

Nat lifted her brush away from the bulkhead and glanced over her shoulder at Isin. "Why not? It was already gold. The two colors go great together." She'd uncovered the paint machine in the utility room on D deck three days after they'd arrived in their mountain camp. It would have been a practical necessity on a ship carrying commercial passengers. The crew wouldn't want the cost of a maintenance layover for cosmetic fixes they could make themselves.

He grimaced. "But it's so... so...."

"Dramatic? Vibrant? Stunning?" She gave him an innocent smile.

His frown deepened. "Gaudy. It will draw attention."

"Is that a problem? Red's a fearsome color. Aren't mercenaries supposed to look fearsome?"

"But you only painted the top line and the front edge of the wings. It makes the ship look like a weird bird."

"A phoenix, to be exact." She stepped aside so he could see the name she'd painted onto the bulkhead. She'd chosen the location with great care—directly across from the ladder leading to the upper hatch. The spot where it had all begun.

"*Phoenix*?" He stared at the red and gold swirls of paint, and the list of names underneath. The names of the deceased crew. She'd compiled them from the ship's logs.

His gaze swung back to her. "You want to name the ship *Phoenix?*"

"Correction. I've *named* the ship *Phoenix*. Pete and Marlin are onboard with it, and Kenji likes it, too. I didn't bother asking Shash, because she'd say no just to spite me."

His brows drew down, shadowing his eyes. "You didn't ask me."

"You said you didn't care."

"About the *paint!* I didn't know a name came with it."

She set the brush down and faced him. "So you don't like the name?"

"That's not the point. You—"

"So you *do* like it?"

"You're missing the—"

"No, I'm not. Do you like the name or not?"

His lips pressed together as he glowered at her.

She didn't budge. "Do you like it?"

Slowly, the belligerence faded, the corners of his mouth tilting up. "I like it."

"Great."

"But you shouldn't have made the decision without talking to me."

"You made the decision to fix the cannons without talking to me."

"That's different."

"Why?"

"Because we needed defenses for the ship."

"I agree. You could have asked Kenji to work on the shields. You chose to focus on offensive weapons instead."

"And I'll be doing it again as soon as we reach our next destination. We need to be prepared to repel hostile forces."

She folded her arms. "You're assuming this ship will be used for mercenary work. I didn't agree to that."

He mirrored her pose. "I can't let you take the ship."

"*Let* me?" She jabbed a finger at his chest. "You don't have the right to *let* me do anything. You still owe me."

He captured her wrist between his fingers, preventing her from poking him. "Natasha, we've been over this. If you take this ship, my crew will hunt you down. I can't–"

"What if I hired them to run freight instead? *Phoenix* could use a larger crew."

"They're mercenaries, not cargo haulers."

"What difference does it make if they're making money?"

"Freight doesn't pay as well as mercenary work."

"But they won't have to kill people. I don't want to pilot for a crew of killers who leave a trail of bodies in their wake."

His grip on her wrist tightened. "Is that how you see me? As a killing machine?"

His question made her pause. She'd certainly seen him that way when he'd first arrived in the dunes. But her view of him had changed quite a bit since then. She didn't fear him anymore. And that said a lot.

She gave him the most honest answer she could. "Sometimes." He certainly didn't need weapons strapped to his hip to look lethal.

"And the rest of the time?"

"The rest of the time you're... Isin." Neither friend nor foe, a nebulous walking contradiction that kept her continually off balance.

He released her wrist and stepped back. "And you don't want to work for the killer or... the other."

"No, I don't."

He frowned. "Do you really dislike me that much?"

She blinked. "Of course not. It has nothing to do with liking or disliking you."

"It doesn't?"

She shook her head. "I've spent my entire life working under the heel of someone else's boot. I want to run my *own* life for a change. This ship is my ticket to freedom."

The lines on his face smoothed out. "I see." His gaze grew thoughtful as he studied her. "What if we make a deal?"

"What kind of deal?"

"As soon as the repairs are finished, we'll take *Phoenix* and *Vengeance* to an outpost where we can both look for work. We'll set a minimum bid, and whoever lands a job that meets that bid first, whether it's hauling freight or a mercenary mission, takes command of both ships until the job is done."

Nat stared at him. Surely she'd misheard. "You mean if I find a freight job that will pay the minimum bid before you find a mercenary job, I'll command both *Phoenix* and *Vengeance* until the delivery is complete?"

"That's right. Since freight pays less, you'd have to find a larger freight haul that requires the use of two ships in order to meet the minimum." He lifted a brow. "But if I find a mercenary job first, you'll be under my command as pilot for this ship until the job is done."

She licked her lips. It was a tantalizing proposition. She stood to make a lot of money. And if she won, she'd be in control of not just this ship, but his, too. He'd be working for her. "What bid amount did you have in mind?"

He named a figure.

Her chest constricted. She'd never even envisioned that much money.

"Too rich for your blood?"

She bit the inside of her cheek to hold back her knee-jerk response. "No. That's fine." By hook or by crook, she was going to win this wager. "But I want to choose our destination."

His eyes narrowed. "Which is?"

"Gallows Edge."

Thirty-One

"Interstellar engines are primed and ready, Nat."

"Thanks, Pete." Nat pulled up the computations for the interstellar jump and entered them into *Phoenix*'s navigational system as Troi disappeared from view in the ship's aft camera.

Isin sat in the tactical chair, monitoring the sensor readings and comm.

His presence beside her for this flight felt both familiar and strange. The last time they'd been in the black together, the arrival of a Setarip cruiser had changed the course of their lives forever. "Any ships up ahead?"

"We're all clear." He met her gaze. "No Setarips."

So his thoughts were running along the same line as hers. Neither of them wanted a repeat of that experience. "Good to know." She double-checked her display's status indicators. Pete and Shash had both signed off on the ship's readiness for space flight, but since this was *Phoenix*'s first voyage off world, a little hyper-vigilance seemed appropriate.

"The shields and weapons systems are online, too," he continued. "Kenji's fine tuning the calibrations. If we need them, we'll be ready."

"Glad to hear it." Not that she planned to get into any firefights in the near future. She glanced at the chronometer. Five minutes to the jump window. "Is *Vengeance* still waiting for us in the next system?"

Isin nodded. "Itorye's had the crew scrubbing the ship from bow to stern over the last few days. They'll be eager to reach Gallows Edge."

Eager. Not a word she associated with Gallows Edge. How ironic that the outpost she despised with every fiber of her being could become the treasure trove that would push her one step closer to her goal. That is, if she won the bet with Isin. "How fast is *Vengeance?*"

He glanced at her. "Are you afraid they'll beat you there?"

Yes. "No." For all she knew, he'd sent them ahead to gain an advantage. "Will they?"

The hint of a smile curved his lips. "The way you fly? I seriously doubt it."

She narrowed her eyes. "I'm going to take that as a compliment."

"You should. Besides, I gave Itorye orders to wait for us before approaching the outpost." His expression sobered. "Gallows Edge can be rough."

As if that was news to her. Hardly. "I can handle it."

"You've been there before?"

"Yes." And she wasn't going to say any more on the subject. Not yet, anyway.

"Hmm." He settled back into his chair. "Just so you know, we'll be sticking together while we're there."

"Oh, will we?" That hadn't been part of their agreement.

"Yes. One way or another, we'll be working as a team after this. I don't want any surprises."

"From our potential employers? Or from me?"

"Either."

She shrugged. "That's fine. I don't like surprises." In fact, she'd had enough surprises to last a lifetime.

Which is why she was planning ahead. She was playing chess against a master. Selecting Gallows Edge as the target was her best opening gambit, but she'd have to keep her wits about her if she wanted to win. "Approaching the jump window."

"All systems are go," he confirmed.

The vibration though the deck changed subtly as the interstellar engines came online.

She glanced at him.

He was watching her.

"Just so you know, I'm going to win this bet."

The light of battle glowed in his dark eyes. "We'll see."

Oh, yes. They would. "Let the games begin."

Elhadj Isin gets caught between a rock and a starship in MARKED MERCENARIES, book two in the Starhawke Rogue trilogy.

Natasha turned her head to meet Isin's gaze. The message in that look was loud and clear. *Don't mess this up.*

He inclined his head slightly before refocusing his attention on the woman. "I'm Elhadj Isin. Natasha's... associate."

The woman glanced between them. Again, he had the sensation of being visually dissected. "Abbey Green."

And I'm the head of the Galactic Fleet. He'd been in this situation enough times to have anticipated she'd give him an alias. He also picked up on a slight accent, one she was trying very hard to conceal. Paired with her coloring, he'd guess she had roots in southeastern Asia.

"She's looking to hire a couple ships." Natasha's mouth tilted up like the cat who'd eaten the canary. "For a cargo run."

Several earthy swear words swirled behind Isin's tongue, but he kept them contained by taking a drink from the mug Doohan had delivered. He hadn't lost this fight yet. "What's the destination?" If it was nearby, the job might not meet the agreed upon minimum.

Natasha glanced back at Green, whose gaze settled on Isin.

Her eyes narrowed. Ignoring the question, she posed one of her own. "What's your role in this operation?"

A negotiation. He could play this game with his eyes closed. "I'm captain of *Vengeance.* A mercenary warship."

"They provide muscle when needed." Natasha shot him another warning look. "I'm captain of *Phoenix*. The passenger freighter I mentioned."

Green glanced between them, assessing. "I see."

"We can split up the cargo between the two ships if necessary, depending on what you need transported."

Green pinned Isin with a hard stare. "How many on your crew?"

"Twenty-one."

"All mercenaries?"

"Except for my medic."

"And is your crew loyal? Trustworthy?"

Isin met her stare for stare. "As long as they get paid."

Green's lips pursed, her gaze shifting to Natasha. "And what about your crew?"

"Definitely trustworthy. We're not mercenaries. We're freight runners."

The silent condemnation in her tone loosened Isin's tongue. "And smugglers and thieves."

Natasha kicked his leg with the heel of her boot. "Only if the job requires it."

Captain's Log

It started as a simple cargo delivery...

And then the Setarips attacked. Experience the pulse-pounding adventure on Troi that led to the discovery of the *Phoenix* and Nat's capture by the Setarips in ROGUE, a Starhawke Rogue prequel. Check out my website for information on how to download your free copy!

A series is born

I never set out to write this series. In fact, Natasha Orlov wasn't even part of the original storyline in the Starhawke universe. Her character appeared during the writing of book three in the Starhawke Rising series, THE HONOR OF DECEIT. Initially, she was going to be a minor player, but by the time that story was completed, she'd proven to be so much more.

When I agreed to write a short story for an anthology featuring unlikely heroes, I knew Nat fit the bill perfectly. It was during the development of that story that she introduced me to Isin (pronounced EYE-sin). Their dynamic fascinated me, and sparked all kinds of questions. Why did Nat risk her life to save him? Did he survive the Setarip attack? What happened to him during the year of Nat's captivity? Did Nat ever return to the ship to look for him?

Discovering the answers to those questions led to the book you're holding in your hands, and the launch of this series. I hope you have as much fun reading it as I've had writing it!

Marlin and Pete

These two are near and dear to my heart. Marlin's character was influenced by the talented actor Albert Brooks, who excels at portraying Eeyore-like characters you can't help but love and root for, including his namesake in *Finding Nemo*. Marlin's the type of guy who will look for a dark cloud on a sunny day.

Pete is his perfect foil. While Marlin's reality is rooted in fear, Pete has an unshakable core of strength that keeps him grounded. His character is loosely based on a friend of mine, who also share's Pete's heart of gold and deep sense of loyalty. It's impossible for me to imagine the *Phoenix* taking flight without him.

The Phoenix

Have you ever tried to bury a ship in the sand and keep it hidden? It proved to be more challenging than I'd imagined.

First, I had to figure out why no one had discovered the ship before Nat and Isin stumbled over it. Research provided the ground mineralization concept, which helped with camouflaging both the *Phoenix* and *Gypsy*, while also allowing for the ship to be close enough to the dune's surface that Nat could trip over the upper hatch.

The fate of the original crew was another puzzle that needed a solution, since I couldn't have the ship in pieces, but I also couldn't leave any survivors from the crash. That meant shorting out the ship's communication system and asphyxiating the crew so they never made it off the ship.

But the greatest stumbling point I hit was how the ship was positioned in the dunes. That might seem like a minor point, but I had to take into account how it landed, how the sand had shifted to cover it, and how the ship's hull shape would affect the dunes. And I still got it wrong the first time. A dear friend pointed out to me during a beta read that the angle of tilt I'd originally specified for the ship would have made the stairs completely impassable. Kind of a problem when they're the only way to get between decks.

When it came to detailing the ship's interior layout, Nat stepped up to the plate to guide the process. She had very specific ideas of how her ship looked, especially the compact bridge. Whenever I strayed off course, she'd hit me with a quip or comment that brought me back on track. Or she'd walk into the section of the ship in question and start showing me what I needed to know.

As for the ship's name, I'd had it in mind for a while – it just seemed like a natural fit for a ship rising out of a sea of hot, dry sand. But Nat's the one who decided to add the red paint, giving the ship its distinctive flair. I learned long ago not to argue when my characters get an idea in their heads, especially when they have a gleam in their eyes and they're holding a brush dripping with red paint.

Enjoy the journey!
Audrey

P.S. – I always write to music, so if you'd like to experience this story the way that I did, listen to the film score for *Raiders of the Lost Ark* while you read.

Audrey Sharpe grew up believing in the Force and dreaming of becoming captain of the Enterprise. She's still working out the logistics of moving objects with her mind, but writing science fiction provides a pretty good alternative. When she's not off exploring the galaxy with Aurora and her crew, she lives in the Sonoran Desert, where she has an excellent view of the stars.

For more information about Audrey and the Starhawke universe, visit her website and join the crew!

AudreySharpe.com

CPSIA information can be obtained
at www.ICGtesting.com
Printed in the USA
BVHW030813280819
557032BV00001B/46/P